THE·ORACLE·DOLL

OTHER YEARLING BOOKS YOU WILL ENJOY:

YEARLING BOOKS/YOUNG YEARLINGS/YEARLING CLASSICS
are designed especially to entertain and enlighten young people. Charles F. Reasoner, Professor Emeritus of Children's Lit-
erature and Reading, New York University, is consultant to this
series.

For a complete listing of all Yearling titles,
write to Dell Readers Service,
P.O. Box 1045, South Holland, Illinois 60473.

THE ·ORACLE · DOLL

CATHERINE · DEXTER

A Yearling Book

Published by
Dell Publishing
a division of
The Bantam Doubleday Dell Publishing Group, Inc.
666 Fifth Avenue
New York, New York 10103

The trademark Yearling® is registered in the U.S. Patent and Trademark Office.

ISBN: 0-440-40114-3

Printed in the United States of America

Reprinted by arrangement with Macmillan Publishing Company

December 1988

10 9 8 7 6 5 4 3 2 1

CW

For Anna and Emily

THE · ORACLE · DOLL

CHAPTER · 1

Rose Wilson sat blissfully alone at the breakfast table. She was looking out the window, letting the sun pour in on her face and soaking up its sleepy warmth. It was so peaceful right now in the kitchen. The window looked out onto nothing special—just the Wilsons' driveway, busy with birds and a stray cat. A cyclone fence separated the driveway from their neighbors' yard. Through the diamond spaces of the fence, Rose could see the Smiths' little round barbecue and their picnic table, with the salt and pepper shakers still sitting on it. She could hear the voices of Mr. and Mrs. Smith coming through the open windows. They didn't have any children.

Not that she cared, anyway. There was nobody for Rose to play with in the neighborhood, unless you counted Rose's younger sister Lucy—which you couldn't. There was also James Leon Handry, but she and James were not friends. It didn't matter to Rose. She liked being by herself early on this summer morning, one of many that were stretching ahead. No one hurried her along, no one nagged at her to collect her homework and remember her lunch box and brush her own hair, now that she was ten. She could just sit in her nightgown and watch beads of water run down the sides of the cold glass milk bottle. She could just sit and stare out the window. When she sat close to the screen, she could make her eyes blur back and forth, now looking at the driveway and seeing the screen as a blur, now focusing on the tiny grids of the screen and making the background a blur. Now she saw the leaves on the honeysuckle bush, now she didn't. Now she saw the creamy blossoms, now they slid to a whitish haze.

"Rose, you're going to get a smudge on your nose," said an impatient voice. "Furthermore, you may just push that screen right out of its frame."

Rats! Here came the sergeant on patrol. As usual.

"I have some errands to do this morning, and I'd like you to get on with your breakfast so I can clean up before we leave."

Errands. As usual. Hurry, hurry, hurry. Do this, do that. All Rose wanted to do was sit in one place and not bother anyone. She didn't move, feeling enveloped in stillness as the sun streamed in.

"I don't see any action, Rose," her mother went on. She was rinsing things at the kitchen sink, going back and forth to the counters, her clogs thunking on the floor. Her mother was a morning person, as Rose had heard many times. "I never was one before, but I've become one," she would say, looking significantly at her children.

Rose herself was not a morning person. She wasn't much of an evening person either. She didn't know what part-of-the-day person she was.

"Okay," Rose said. "All *right*." She pulled back from the window and turned to the yellow pottery bowl in front of her. It was full of raisin bran. "Are there any strawberries?"

"We finished them all last night," said her mother. "How about a banana?"

"I guess." Rose didn't like bananas as much as strawberries. Last week Lucy had had strawberries all over her birthday cake. She had turned five.

"Now Rose, I hope you aren't going to let this entire day go to waste," her mother went on. "How about riding that bike of yours? Or roller-skating?"

"Maybe," Rose poured milk on her cereal and fiddled with her spoon. "Can't I just rest?"

"The Russells might go swimming. That would be a nice outing." Rose's mother gave her a smile that was also a question. Will you please go swimming with the other kids? Will you please do something, and not sit around all the time?

Rose's mother hadn't used to fuss at her to do things with other kids. But she had gotten pretty bad on the subject during the past year, when Rose was in fifth grade. She had gotten crosser about everything, in fact, saying they should never have moved to this old heap of a house, and why were the children always underfoot, and things like that. Sometimes she was her old self again, being silly, making faces with Rose, giving her hugs for no good reason, talking in made-up accents. She had short curly brown hair that was always out of combing, and brown eyes that were just like Rose's (Lucy had them, too). She thought she was a little too fat, but Rose thought she looked very nice, especially when she was dressed up.

The banana must have been sitting beside Rose's plate for a while when she noticed it. Her mother had whisked out of the kitchen, and now here she was, back again, saying good-by to Rose's father. He stooped down to kiss Rose, tickling her with his moustache. He was wearing the green tie she had given him for his birthday. He smelled good, like soap and pipe tobacco. " 'Bye, Daddy," she said.

"I want a kiss!" screeched Lucy, standing in the doorway. Of course her sister would come down, right at that moment. She was holding her new doll, a birthday present. It was a talking doll, with a voice box run by a battery. It talked every time it was moved. Tilt it to the left, it said "Ma-ma." Tilt it to the right, it hiccupped. Sometimes it even talked when it wasn't moved. A couple of days ago Rose had walked into the kitchen, and suddenly from under the table a voice had said "Hi-ya!" Lucy had left Gabriella on the floor, and the vibrations from Rose's footsteps had started her voice box.

" 'Bye, dearie," said Mr. Wilson, kissing Lucy.

"Uh-oh!" said the doll.

Mr. Wilson picked up his briefcase and vanished down the back steps. Rose listened to his footsteps fade away.

"Let's get on with breakfast, Lucy," Mrs. Wilson said. "I've got errands to do."

"Goody! Can Gabby come?" cried Lucy. That was

the nickname she had given her doll.

"Hiccup!" said Gabriella.

"Yes, she can. But let's get moving."

Rose looked in dismay at her bowl of uneaten cereal, now totally milk-logged.

"Do I have to eat this?" she asked.

"Oh, Rose." Her mother sounded exasperated.

Rose poured the soggy flakes down the sink and reached for the cereal box.

There is nothing worse than doing errands on a summer's day. Anyone would rather go swimming, or see a movie, or sleep late, or eat ice cream in the morning, or read comic books, or just lie down under a tree and wait for someone to ask you if anything is wrong. But by eight-thirty Mrs. Wilson had efficiently herded both Rose and Lucy into the car. The air was steamy. The car was stuffy. Rose rolled down her window as fast as she could.

"This car stinks," she said. Leaning out the window, she could see James Leon Handry walking up the side-walk to meet his bus for camp. He was carrying a yellow lunch box and a blue wad that was probably his swimming towel with his bathing suit inside it. James was a year older than Rose, though he was shorter than she was, and his mother let him do all kinds of things by himself. He could take the streetcar alone, and he could walk down Center Street as far as he liked, and he could ride his bike in the street. He could even hang around the schoolyard if he wanted to. Mrs. Wilson didn't approve. She said that James was allowed to do all those things because his mother was never home and his father lived in California. He was always with a baby-sitter, and no one took the trouble to really look after him.

Rose often saw James's regular baby-sitter coming up the street in the afternoon. She always waved to Rose and Lucy if they were on their front steps. Her name was Cindy, and she looked really nice. She was very pretty, and she had the best clothes, including a collection of jellies, transparent plastic sandals, in all different colors. Rose couldn't imagine that she wasn't taking enough trouble looking after James. James looked fine to Rose. But she wouldn't have dared to try to be friends with him. Whenever they saw each other on the street, they looked the other way.

Rose flapped her braids, one of which was tighter than the other, and jostled Lucy, partly on purpose. Lucy's plump shoulder was sticky. "Yuck!" said Rose.

"Ma-ma!" said Lucy's doll.

"How come Lucy has to bring her doll?" asked Rose. Lucy had also brought her new red tote bag that had her name on it. She had crammed it full of doll clothes and little wads of leaves that were her pretend money. The leaves were smooth and oval shaped, and they had an interesting smell. Lucy had picked them from a bush in the Wilsons' backyard. The smell made Rose all the more impatient at being shut up in the car.

"Why do we always have to go on errands? Why can't I just stay home?"

"We'll do them as fast as we can," Mrs. Wilson said over her shoulder, as she backed the car down the driveway. "There's only the cleaners, the hardware store, some birthday wrapping paper, and the groceries."

"Only! But that's a million! We'll be doing them all day!"

"I promise you we won't," said her mother.

"Hi-ya!" said Lucy's doll.

Lucy gazed out the window and peacefully sucked her thumb.

The cleaners came first. Mrs. Wilson parked the car on Center Street. While she was putting coins into the meter, Rose stood on the sidewalk and looked in the windows of Dolores's Fine Dresses. The sign over the door said "Dresses for Special Occasions." The dresses were bright colors, pink and green, and made with fluffy net skirts and sequins. Rose wondered who bought them, because the store was always closed and iron grates were fastened across the big windows. The same headless model was always on display in the same yellow strapless dress. Rose decided that someday she would buy that dress for herself. It looked as though it would still be there when she grew up.

"Rose, let's move along," said her mother.

"Don't you like this dress, Mom?" she asked.

"Hmm, well, it certainly is bright, isn't it?" her mother said.

As they stepped off the curb, a creaky voice right beside them suddenly said, WATCH IT! Rose looked up and saw a taxi speeding straight toward them. Mrs. Wilson jumped back to the curb, yanking Rose and Lucy with her. The taxi shot past, barely missing them and blowing exhaust fumes into their faces.

"What a jerk!" said Rose, badly frightened. Little whirlwinds of grit swirled around her toes.

"Thank goodness you saw that," Mrs. Wilson said, turning to Lucy. "Dearie, that was a very close call. You warned us just in time." Her voice was shaky, and she was suddenly out of breath.

Lucy looked up at her mother. Rose knew she hadn't said a thing, but Lucy didn't explain. "P.U." was all she said, and sniffed the exhaust fumes hanging in the air.

"Ma-ma!" said the doll in a creaky little voice.

An hour later, Mrs. Wilson had almost finished her errands. Clean suits and dresses rustled in plastic bags on the front seat. She had accumulated two brown bags full of light bulbs, a bucket of paint for the porch floor, and a glass bread pan from Harry's Hardware. She had let Rose and Lucy pick out the wrapping paper in the gift shop, two packages each: Mickey Mouse, Pac-Man, pink paper with girls wearing pink old-fashioned dresses, and blue paper with girls wearing blue old-fashioned dresses. The paper was for the supplies drawer, to be on hand for the next birthday. Rose had wanted to buy a ballerina Smurf, too, but her mother said definitely not. Rose was sulking in the back seat.

"Grocery shopping's the very last thing we have to do," Mrs. Wilson said, as she drove into the supermarket parking lot. The asphalt acres glistened with heat. "I know you're tired and hot," she went on, "but it will be air-conditioned inside the store."

"Can I get gum? Can I get bubble gum, raspberry bubble gum, please, please, please, just this once?" begged Rose.

"Me, too, but I want strawberry," said Lucy.

"Sugar gum is bad for your teeth," said Mrs. Wilson. She pulled on the emergency brake and slid out of the driver's seat. "You don't need to roll up the windows, it's too hot," she told them. Her shopping list fell to the pavement. The children got out of the car.

"We never get bubble gum, and it's my favorite, just this once, please," Rose went on.

"Sugar-free gum is better for your teeth," her mother said. She groaned and stooped down to retrieve the list from under the car.

"Bubble gum," said Lucy.

"Bubble gum," said Rose.

The grocery list blew away again. "Well, I suppose you won't get cavities from one pack of gum," their mother said. "Just this once, if you'll be quiet and not fight while I do my shopping." She trapped the list under her sandal, picked it up, and put it in her skirt pocket.

"My doll!" Lucy turned back to the car.

"Lucy, no one will take it." Mrs. Wilson was starting to sound exasperated again.

"I want to bring her. And I need her stuff, too."

"Then you'll have to carry everything yourself, the whole way." Lucy nodded. Mrs. Wilson fished the doll and the tote bag from the back seat, and they started across the parking lot. Heat rose from the blacktop, and the blazing sun struck their faces. "Now what will we eat today?" Mrs. Wilson asked, thinking out loud.

CANTALOUPE, said a scratchy voice on her left, the side where Lucy was walking.

Rose glanced up and saw a banner taped inside the window of the supermarket. Huge blue letters read "Jersey Cantaloupe, Three For One Dollar."

"Cantaloupe!" repeated Mrs. Wilson, smiling down. "What a good idea." Lucy and Rose looked at each other in a funny way. "Cantaloupe is a long word. I didn't know you could read that well, Lucy."

Lucy looked up at her mother and hitched her doll securely under one arm.

"She can't," said Rose.

By the time they finished the errands, it was too hot to do anything, even play Sorry or Old Maid. Lucy went into her parents' air-conditioned bedroom and climbed on the bed. She took her doll with her.

Mrs. Wilson's friend Anita Russell dropped by and offered to take Rose swimming with her own children at the YMCA. The Russells had lived on the Wilsons' street until a year ago, when they had moved to another neighborhood. They were still in Boston, but their new neighborhood was across the parkway, up on a hill, where there were lots of big houses with big yards. They had moved not a moment too soon, in Rose's opinion. She could see Charlie and Megan Russell looking gloomily out of the wayback of their station wagon. Their faces were red and sweaty.

"No, thanks," said Rose.

"Are you sure?" asked her mother, with Anita standing right there. "You'd be cooler, dearie, and it's so nice of Anita to take you along."

"I have a heat headache." Rose had recently seen a program on television about heat lightning.

"Goodness—why didn't you say so?" Rose knew her mother didn't like to appear neglectful in front of other parents. "Let's look for an aspirin."

The Russells waved good-by. Rose watched Charlie and Megan through the wayback as the station wagon drove away. Their faces, pressed against the window, got smaller and smaller until they were just two fuzzy pink circles.

"My headache is gone now," Rose said as her mother began sorting through the medicine bottles in the hall closet. Mrs. Wilson looked at Rose suspiciously. Rose shrugged her shoulders.

Mrs. Wilson pressed her hand to Rose's forehead. "You don't feel hot," she said.

Rose pulled away. "I'm going outside to read," she said. She gathered up her paperback mysteries from behind the television set in the kitchen and went out the patio door. An old picnic blanket was crumpled in a heap on the stone table that stood, on not-quite-even legs, far back in the tangle of greenery that stretched behind the Wilsons' house. Rose shook out the blanket and spread it under the cherry tree. She lay back comfortably, but she didn't open any of her books—as soon as her head touched the ground, she remembered about the doll. She definitely had heard it say something it shouldn't have been able to say. For one fleeting, crazy moment, Lucy's doll had sounded alive.

After supper the heat still hung thick in the air. It was like eating dinner in a shower room: Everything was sticky and damp. Her mother asked Rose to clear the table, and when she stood up, she practically had to peel herself away from her chair.

They had cantaloupe for dessert. "Can we go to Bill's Ice Cream?" Lucy asked with her mouth full. "Please, please? Can we get ice cream?"

"Can Lucy and I go by ourselves?" Rose asked. "We can count our own change."

Mr. Wilson looked inquiringly at Mrs. Wilson, for he left these decisions to her. She shook her head. "It's not safe," she said, as she always did. "Particularly crossing at that corner."

"But James's mother lets him!"

"I don't do things the way James's mother does."

"Let's all go then," said Mr. Wilson in a falsely cheerful voice.

Rose groaned. "When are you ever going to say I can go somewhere by myself?"

"That's a tricky question," her mother said.

"It's not tricky," Rose squawked. "I don't see anything dangerous about going there. I wish I did! At least it would be interesting."

"I haven't had a peach ice-cream cone for ages," Mr. Wilson said. "Let's go right now."

"Goody!" cried Lucy. She grabbed up her doll and her bag, and they went out the back door.

The sky was still light. Across the parkway, on one side of the hill in the park, men in blue T-shirts were playing softball. Behind them Rose could see the pond gleaming under the evening sky. In the Grass Bowl, members of a rock band gave off loud twangs as they plugged in their guitars and loud speakers and got ready for an outdoor concert. Stray dogs trotted up the sidewalk with their tongues hanging out, and couples, a few of them dressed like punks, strolled toward the park. The Wilsons' street was lined with two-family houses. Very old people lived by themselves in some of the houses, and groups of students and working people lived in others. Because there were so many strangers and different kinds of people going up and down their street, the Wilson parents didn't let Rose and Lucy go anywhere by themselves. "When you're older," they would say. "This is the city, after all."

James and his mother lived on the first floor of a yellow house halfway down the block. As they passed it, Rose could see James sitting alone in his living room, watching television. Bluish light was reflected onto his face. He had propped his bare feet up over the arm of his chair, and he was scratching the back of his knee with one toe. Rose felt embarrassed and a little bit sad to be watching him when he didn't know it. He looked kind of lonely.

Mrs. Wilson had gone on to the next house and was standing by its tiny side yard. "Would you just look at Mr. Pitts's lettuces," she said. They looked at Mr. Pitts's lettuces. Two pale green rows of them glowed in the twilight. As they were standing there, a hush fell over the street—no cars were passing at that moment—and in the silence an insect buzzed and twanged in a bush. Then a small, tinny voice said, HELLO, DORIS.

Mrs. Wilson, whose name was not Doris, looked around briefly. "I don't know how he does it in such a small space," she went on. Rose looked around her father at Lucy, and Lucy looked back at Rose. Neither of them said anything, but they both glanced at the doll dangling from Lucy's free hand.

Bill's Homemade Ice Cream was on the other side of Center Street, between a Greek pizza shop and a beauty parlor. Bill's was new. It had a polished wood floor, and green plants hung in the window. Posters of old-time ice-cream sodas decorated the walls. The air conditioning was cool and delicious as it circulated around Rose's ears. A man wearing one gold earring and a long white apron and two girls with long, loose hair and white aprons were scooping out ice cream.

"Strawberry, no jimmies," said Rose.

"I want chocolate and a lot of jimmies," said Lucy.

Mr. Wilson got peach, and Mrs. Wilson ordered chocolate chip. They teased out handfuls of paper napkins from the metal napkin dispenser. Outside in the heat again, their ice cream began to melt. As they stood on the corner, waiting for the Walk light and licking frantically around their cones, a bus pulled up and flapped open its doors. Among the riders that climbed off, Rose saw a familiar figure. There was Mrs. Donahue, their old neighbor and baby-sitter. She had taken care of them when they were little. Mrs. Wilson saw her, too, and called out, "Hello, Doris!"

Lucy trotted right over to be kissed, but Rose just stood there. She just stood there, staring like a hypnotized person at Lucy's doll.

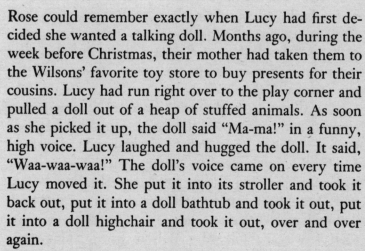

CHAPTER 2

Rose could remember exactly when Lucy had first decided she wanted a talking doll. Months ago, during the week before Christmas, their mother had taken them to the Wilsons' favorite toy store to buy presents for their cousins. Lucy had run right over to the play corner and pulled a doll out of a heap of stuffed animals. As soon as she picked it up, the doll said "Ma-ma!" in a funny, high voice. Lucy laughed and hugged the doll. It said, "Waa-waa-waa!" The doll's voice came on every time Lucy moved it. She put it into its stroller and took it back out, put it into a doll bathtub and took it out, put it into a doll highchair and took it out, over and over again.

Lucy pulled on her mother's hand. "I want this doll for Christmas."

"But dear, you've already made up your list for Santa Claus," said Mrs. Wilson.

"I want this one."

"How about for your birthday?"

"That's too long! Can we get her right now?"

"No, Lucy. I'm not going to buy you a doll right now. But if you still want it when your birthday comes, you can have it as a birthday present. I promise you."

Rose, listening to this from the rows of teddy bears in the next aisle, held her breath, half expecting Lucy to burst out crying. But Lucy had merely nodded her head.

"My daughter is very interested in this doll," Mrs. Wilson said to the clerk.

The clerk smiled brightly. "It's a great doll. We've sold dozens like her. You can wash her in the washing machine, you can shampoo her hair. The voice box zips out in the back, so you can replace the battery. And she'll never stop talking."

"I see." Mrs. Wilson turned the doll over and smoothed out a cloth tag sewn into its back seam. "It says here that she's named Gabriella."

Mrs. Wilson handed the doll back to Lucy and looked along the shelves behind the clerk's counter. "Oh, look at those. Look at those lovely ones with handmade dresses and hand-knitted sweaters." Some of the dolls on display had china heads and delicate painted cheeks. Mrs. Wilson went behind the counter and picked up a rag doll with embroidered eyelashes and a smile that even Rose thought was adorable. Mrs. Wilson sighed. "This one is very expensive, of course," she said. "The other one is more practical for a young child." Gabriella had stiff blond vinyl hair and a plastic face with a fixed smile on it, and she didn't cost much. Rose could tell at a glance that thousands and thousands of Gabriellas had been manufactured by a doll factory somewhere. There was nothing special about her.

"How about this one?" Mrs. Wilson held the rag doll up for Lucy to see.

Lucy shook her head and hugged the talking doll. That was the way Lucy was. If she loved this doll, she was not going to change her mind.

A few months later, when Lucy's birthday came near, Mrs. Wilson asked Rose if she wanted to come along to help pick out Lucy's promised doll. The toy store was out of Gabriellas, so they drove out to Boodle's, a toy warehouse store, to buy the doll. Boodle's was enormous, so big that people pushed shopping carts around and filled them to the brim with toys. Long aisles of shelves stretched up twice as tall as Mrs. Wilson. By following the overhead signs Rose and her mother found the doll section, and there, at the end of the aisle, were stacks of Gabriellas, all in identical pink boxes with cellophane windows. Some of the Gabriellas had pink skin, some had brown skin. Some had black hair, some had blond hair. Their faces were all the same.

"How will we ever pick one?" said Mrs. Wilson, examining the doll on the top. "They must be the same, but let's be sure." She took down the first box, then the next box, and then the box beneath that. Glancing at each one, Rose began to think that the faces did not seem exactly alike after all. She had a feeling she would know when they had found the right one. Mrs. Wilson stacked boxes around her on the floor: two more boxes, and two more after that, and two more after that. "Goodness!"

she said finally. "Why don't you decide?"

The next doll was the right one. Rose knew it as soon as she saw the face. This doll had a lively look, though her dress was squashed and wrinkled from being packed and there was smudge on her nose. "This is it," Rose said, and she handed it to her mother. The box bore a conspicuous message across its front: Battery Not Included.

Mrs. Wilson restacked the other boxes on the shelf, and they made their way to the front of the store. Mrs. Wilson picked up a 9-volt battery in the check-out line, paid for the doll and the battery, and had the cashier staple the whole bundle into a plain brown bag. When they got home, Rose's mother hid the bag in her closet.

"We can't forget the doll," said Rose the night before Lucy's birthday. She was in her parents' bedroom, helping to wrap birthday presents and trying not to feel cross. Rose's own birthday was so far away, and she knew that at the very moment when Lucy was getting her presents and liking every single one of them, she herself would be thinking of hundreds of things that she wanted but didn't have. She just couldn't help thinking of them: a new live dog or a horse or a ten-speed bicycle or a dollhouse with electric lights. Anyhow, she didn't want a doll. She had outgrown dolls—at least she had thought she had until now. Now she felt a taste of sour envy, like a spoonful of vinegar on the back of her tongue. She had never had a talking doll.

"Can I put the battery in?" she asked her mother.

"I'm not sure where it goes," said her mother. "Let's take out the voice box and have a look."

Rose unzipped the back of the doll's cloth body and took out a tan plastic box. The back of it snapped off easily. Two curly wires sprang out. They were fastened together at the end by a plastic cap. One of the wires was purple and one was yellow.

"How odd," said Mrs. Wilson. "I've never seen wires like these. Usually they're red and black."

The battery was packed in a clear plastic bubble glued to a cardboard square. "I'll open it," said Rose. She tore off the cardboard back and shook out the battery. On its top were two silver terminals that she could tell would snap onto the plastic cap joining the wires. She fitted everything together, tucked in the wires, and pressed the battery into its slot. As the battery clicked in, Rose heard a strange sound, something she couldn't identify then, though she remembered it later. It sounded like a quick rush of air, as though someone had taken a deep breath. Rose popped the cover of the voice box back in place.

"Ma-ma!" said the voice box, right in Rose's hand. It had a funny voice, high and tinny, that sounded like a cartoon chipmunk or a record on the wrong speed.

Rose and her mother couldn't help laughing.

"Hi-ya!" the box said next.

They waited. A whirring sound followed, and then the box gave a crying noise: "Waa-waa-waa!" It hiccupped. Finally it said, "Uh-oh!"

Rose and Mrs. Wilson laughed again. Rose began to feel better. She put the voice box back into the body of the doll and pulled up the zipper. She turned Gabriella right side up and brushed out her yellow Dutch hair. "She looks better with her hair fluffed up," Rose said.

Every time she tilted Gabriella in a new direction, the doll spoke.

Rose knew Lucy was going to love the doll. "I think Lucy's going to be old enough to share now," she said hopefully.

Her mother gave her a pat on the shoulder. "I know you'll have a turn with the doll. You'll have to be patient, though. Just remember how you feel about your new things on your birthday."

"I will, I will," Rose groaned, gritting her teeth.

All during Lucy's birthday dinner, the package on the sideboard talked. It was wrapped in glittery paper, and it was the shape of a box of boots. But Lucy knew that boots did not cry or say "Ma-ma!"

After she had blown out her birthday candles and her mother had cut pieces of cake for everyone, she slowly undid the ribbon, unstuck each piece of Scotch tape, and spread the wrapping paper flat. She turned over the pink cardboard box, opened one end, and there, inside, was the doll she had wanted. "Ooh, look!" she said.

"What do you think we're doing?" muttered Rose.

Lucy picked up the doll and looked happily into its blue eyes. The eyes didn't close, but when Lucy wrapped the doll in a piece of cloth and put her down, she looked as if she were sleeping anyhow. She wore a pink dress and a pink sash. She was exactly what Lucy wanted.

"Ma-ma!" the doll said. She sounded just like a baby. Lucy picked her up and put her down, and the doll began to cry "Waa-waa-waa!"

Lucy turned pink. She always blushed when she was

very, very happy. Mrs. Wilson laughed and gave her a hug.

Lucy put the doll into its new pink plastic stroller and pushed it down the hall and through the dining room and around the sun porch, in a long wandering circle that took in the entire circumference of the house.

Rose turned away, disgusted. She could hear the doll's voice all over the house. All that Rose could think was, when will the battery wear out?

Because it was her birthday Lucy was allowed to stay up late, and it was after ten o'clock when she and Rose finally went upstairs. Lucy shoved aside a pile of things—doll clothes, some old leaves she used for pretend money, a deck of cards—to make a place for Gabriella beside the corner of her bureau. Gabriella said, "Ma-ma!"

"You want a dry Pamper, honey?" Lucy asked. One of her birthday presents was a box of Pampers, the newborn size, for her doll. Lucy took out a fresh Pamper and unfolded it. "Mm, smells like baby powder," she said. She fitted it around Gabriella and fastened the tapes at the waist. "Perfect!"

Gabriella said, "Ma-ma!"

Lucy began taking off her own party shoes. Gabriella said, "Hi-ya!" The buckles on the shoes were stiff. Lucy's socks were sticky, and she had to peel them off. She wiggled her bare toes and stared at the lines left by the straps across her feet. Gabriella said, "Waa-waa-waa!"

Rose put on her nightclothes and started into the bathroom to brush her teeth. "That thing's going to talk all night!" she said.

Lucy didn't answer. She dropped her clothes one by

one in a trail across the rug, took her summer pajamas off their hook, and pulled them on. "Ma-ma!" creaked the voice box.

"I wonder if you're going to talk forever, or what," Rose heard Lucy say. Then Rose turned on the water faucet and began furiously brushing and rinsing her teeth, so she didn't hear what the doll said back. But when she had dried her face and come back, she found Lucy frozen, bent over, looking into Gabriella's painted blue eyes. In a moment Lucy picked up the doll, squeezed her far into the back of the closet, and closed the door. There came a muffled "Hiccup!"

"What's the matter?" asked Rose.

"I don't want to hear her anymore," said Lucy.

"Oh," said Rose in surprise. "Me, either. Well, goodnight, Lucy." She heard their father starting up the stairs to tuck them in. "And happy birthday." It was easier to be gracious now that the birthday was nearly over.

The next morning Lucy opened the closet door and cautiously peeked inside. Rose was only half awake, but she heard the doll's cheery greeting from the depths of the closet: "Hi-ya!"

" 'Morning, sweetie," said Lucy.

Rose pressed the pillow over her ears.

For the rest of the week, Lucy played with Gabriella all day and tucked her into bed with her at night, and soon Rose forgot about Gabriella's being stuffed in the closet. Then came the day they did the errands and went to Bill's for ice cream. Then she began to wonder again.

CHAPTER · 3

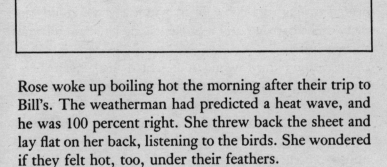

Rose woke up boiling hot the morning after their trip to Bill's. The weatherman had predicted a heat wave, and he was 100 percent right. She threw back the sheet and lay flat on her back, listening to the birds. She wondered if they felt hot, too, under their feathers.

Rose and Lucy shared a large, irregularly shaped room on the third floor of the Wilsons' house. It had been a maid's room long ago and was at the top of a winding staircase that led up from the kitchen. On the second floor of the house was a separate apartment where the Wilsons' tenant, old Mr. Edgar, lived. Mrs. Wilson often talked about redoing the house. Someday, she said, they were going to take part of the second floor so that each girl could have her own room, and they would put in a new kitchen and landscape the yard. But Rose's parents weren't ready to make all these changes yet. Rose knew it had something to do with money. She was just as glad.

She liked the room she had, though she would have preferred not to share it. She liked being on the top floor, where she could peek down from the dormer windows. She loved the backyard the way it was, too—long and skinny and full of overgrown bushes and interesting tangles of weeds. Toward the middle of the yard grew a cherry tree: Rose's favorite place to read was beneath this tree, though the cherry pits scattered on the ground dug into her elbows. At the far end of the yard, beyond the uneven stone table, stood an old garden shed. If she peered through its cobwebbed windows, she could see rusty wheelbarrows and a broken stone bench and some ancient hoes.

Rose sometimes wondered which had been here longer, the garden shed or Mr. Edgar. The Wilsons were glad to have Mr. Edgar for a tenant. He had lived in the second-floor apartment for years and years; no one was sure how long. He had certainly been there since the nuns—or whoever they were—had moved out. But he kept entirely to himself. Mrs. Wilson was always telling Rose and Lucy not to bother Mr. Edgar. He was a recluse, she said. She had no idea how he did his laundry or got his meals. She never saw him carrying groceries. "Maybe he just lives on cottage cheese—or ambrosia, like the gods!" Mrs. Wilson joked. "What's ambrosia?" asked Rose. "When I was in grade school, we used to have something that they called ambrosia in the lunchroom. It was orange slices with coconut." "Ugh," said Rose.

Sometimes the Wilsons heard music upstairs from an instrument that sounded vaguely like a harp. Mr. Wilson said it was probably a record, that he must have a favorite recording he played over and over.

Mr. Edgar had a part-time job at the Children's Museum, Mrs. Wilson explained to Rose. That did not mean that he liked children, however. Rose scarcely ever saw him. He was very thin and bent in the shoulders, and he had pure white hair, bright blue eyes, and olive skin. He didn't look friendly and he didn't look unfriendly. He existed in their lives mostly as a set of footsteps that they heard crossing the kitchen overhead or climbing the front staircase.

Rose's bed was in one of the alcoves in the third-floor room, and when she first woke up every morning, as on this morning, she liked to lie in bed and look out the window, straight into the treetops. Sometimes she imagined herself jumping from the roof to a branch. She could just feel herself soaring up and down that hill of air. She had once told her mother that she wondered what jumping to the branch would feel like. Her mother had gasped and said, "You aren't actually going to try it, are you?"— as if Rose had no common sense at all. Now if Rose had said that to Grandma Foley, her mother's mother, Grandma would probably have smiled and said, "A good deal like hang gliding, I should think."

It was hard for Rose to believe that her mother was Grandma Foley's daughter. Rose's mother was always saying that Rose had too much imagination; she needed "a good dose of reality." And she was always telling Rose to be more down to earth. The way she said "down to earth" made it sound gritty and ground down, like having to walk around with sand in your shoes. The only time that sand in her shoes felt good was when she was on vacation. Last year the Wilsons had gone to an island for a whole month. Rose remembered the long beaches, the salt and the waves, the wild roses, and her mother worrying about ticks. It had smelled so good there. Rose had gone barefoot and turned cartwheels on the huge green lawn of the house they had rented. She had made friends with a girl from Pittsburgh, and every day they met on the same beach and played together.

They were not going back this summer. Her mother said it "wasn't possible" in the same tone of voice that she used when she said that they weren't going to work on the house yet. Rose supposed that her friend from Pittsburgh would look for her at that same beach and wonder where she was. She pictured Ashley carrying her bucket down to the narrow neck of sand between the ocean and the fresh-water pond and climbing the sandy rise and looking and looking for Rose. Rose's forehead got tight with gathering tears just imagining it.

All there was for the Wilsons this summer was swimming at the indoor pool at the Y, which smelled bad, and walking up to dirty old Center Street to get ice cream.

Ice cream. That reminded her. Rose sat up straight and peered over at Lucy's bed, in the other alcove. She saw only Lucy's arm and a fringe of Gabby's blond hair above the line of the sheets.

"Lucy, are you awake?" asked Rose.

"I will be in a minute," said Lucy.

Rose got out of her bed and went to sit on the foot of Lucy's bed. "Now are you?" she asked.

"Almost."

"How's your doll?"

Lucy looked at Rose and said nothing. This was one of Lucy's most annoying habits—not answering when you asked her something.

"Have you heard her say anything funny?" asked Rose.

"I'm not sure," said Lucy.

"Can I hold her for a minute?" asked Rose. She picked Gabby up and tilted her in all directions. Nothing came out but "Ma-ma" and "Waa-waa-waa." Rose had very good hearing, and she knew she had not been mistaken about the extra words. The strangest thing was that what the doll said seemed to be connected with things that happened afterward. Perhaps her mother had bought the wrong battery. Still, how wrong could a battery be?

Up the back stairs from the kitchen came the noise of the refrigerator door opening and closing, dishes rattling, and the television set crackling as it was turned on.

"Breakfast time!" their mother called to them. "We're late. We overslept this morning."

"Hi-ya!" said Gabriella.

Rose and Lucy shed their nightgowns in little heaps on the floor and pulled on shorts and shirts. "Do you remember last night on the way to Bill's?" Rose said in a low voice as they came down the stairs. "Someone said 'HELLO, DORIS'? I think it was her."

"I was wondering," said Lucy. She popped her thumb back in her mouth and clutched Gabriella tighter with her other hand. So two of them had heard it.

Mr. Wilson stood in his shirt sleeves at the kitchen counter pouring cornflakes into a bowl and looking at his watch. The television set was turned on to the channel that gave a one-minute weather forecast. Lucy climbed into her chair and wedged Gabriella in behind her. Rose went over and stood beside her father. "I want cornflakes, too," she said.

"I'm in an awful hurry, sweetie. Here's the bowl, you

can pour them yourself," her father said. He peeled a banana so fast it looked as if it had simply dropped its skin. Slice, slice, slice—disks of banana rustled onto his cornflakes.

Mrs. Wilson came into the kitchen from the dining room, where she had been sorting the laundry. "I'll get their cereal, George. You're in a hurry," she said.

Mr. Wilson began eating while he was walking to the table. He sat down, turned halfway toward the television set to listen to the weather—"sunny in the morning . . . low clouds moving in this afternoon . . . maybe a shower or two tonight"—turned back, and kept eating. He checked his watch again. "Late! Late!" he exclaimed. "There goes James to catch *his* bus."

They caught sight of James going up Dana Street toward the parkway. He was wearing shorts and carrying the same blue wad of a towel. He was talking to himself, and he looked mad. Maybe he hated camp.

Mr. Wilson walked into the dining room, where he had laid his coat and tie over the back of a chair, and began to put on his tie in front of the sideboard mirror. From their places in the kitchen Rose and Lucy watched him tighten the knot of his tie beneath his chin. He seemed to be taking forever. First he tugged his tie one way, then the other, then gave it a little hitch that centered it directly under his Adam's apple. The tie was perfectly placed, smooth and neat, when he was done. He reached for his jacket. Finally, he kissed everyone in his family on the cheek, going from the youngest to the oldest, and walked out the door.

As soon as he was gone, Rose and Lucy finished their

breakfasts at top speed, slurping up the milk in the bottoms of their bowls and practically throwing their dishes into the sink.

"We'll be outside, Mom," Rose called as they ran out the back door.

"Wait a minute!" called their mother. "I want you to finish this cantaloupe." Rose and Lucy hung itchily about while Mrs. Wilson cut the cantaloupe into new-moon-shaped slices. Then they went outside with the juicy pieces and paper napkins and the doll, and they stretched out under the cherry tree. The sun was climbing, and heat could already be felt in the grass and the green leaves around them. Rose heard the dry, rasping repeats of a whirring insect, and in the distance cars whizzed hypnotically by on the parkway. A strong, spicy plant smell was in the air. It was coming from one of the bushes deep in the tangle beside the shed. This particular bush was Rose's favorite secret spot. The bush had grown into a hollow shape, and Rose liked to crawl under the branches and play. It was like being in a fragrant green cave, though sometimes the smell of the leaves was so strong it almost made her dizzy. Early in the spring she had stashed an old metal lunch box under the bush with a few Oreo cookies inside. In the shed she had found a child's three-legged wooden stool, rickety but with some of the paint still on it—red, black, and white. She had put the stool under the bush, too. Beside it she had placed a plastic dish filled with smooth brown pebbles. She and Lucy sometimes used the pebbles for money, sometimes for pretend cooking. Rose felt a little embarrassed still to be playing pretend, but then nobody knew except

Lucy. And Lucy would never tell Charlie and Megan Russell about the green cave. The cave could not be seen, unless a person knew exactly where the entrance was.

Lucy had propped the doll against the trunk of the cherry tree and sat down cross-legged beside her, smacking her lips as she finished her cantaloupe. Rose rolled over onto her back and stared at the leaves overhead and the patterns they made against the blue sky as the wind breathed through the branches. There was such a feeling of sleepy peacefulness in the air. Rose let her eyelids drift down, so that she was looking at the leaves through her eyelashes. Her lashes seemed huge and blurred and transparent. She thought she would never have to move, that she could lie there forever, eating the cherries as they dropped off the tree. The cherries would turn ripe in July, her mother said.

MOTHER'S LEAVING, said a sing-song voice.

Rose opened an eye and lifted her head an inch off the ground. Lucy was sitting perfectly still. Maybe the voice came from a car radio in someone's driveway. You could always hear car radios in summer, when everyone's windows were open. But Rose's heart was beating faster, for she knew it was not a car radio. She put her head down and closed her eyes. It had to be Gabriella.

MOTHER'S LEAVING, the voice repeated. And then it laughed—not a happy laugh, or a good-natured laugh. It was the laugh of someone, or something, who was perfectly sure of herself, or itself.

Rose sat up, completely awake. "She's started again!" she said in a loud whisper to Lucy.

"I know it," said Lucy, who was inching away from

• *30*

the doll. "What's going on with this thing?" she said. "I don't think I like her anymore."

Rose scrutinized the doll's face. Her painted blue eyes stared with a fixed pleasantness. From one angle the eyes seemed to look at her, but from most directions they just looked off somewhere. The doll's pink dress stood out stiffly. Already some dry leaves had stuck in the rickrack.

Rose wondered if she was hearing things. She had read about people having that experience when they were sick. Could she and Lucy both be sick? Or crazy? Fear pricked her scalp. On the other hand, what if she wasn't hearing things? An even bigger prickle rode across her back.

Rose picked the doll up and gently shook her. Only the usual whirring noise and "Ma-ma" came out.

"You want to know something weird?" asked Lucy, who by now had wriggled several feet away from Rose and the doll.

"Oh, Lucy. What do you know about what's weird?" said Rose.

"I know as much as you do about what's weird!"

"Okay. What is it?" Rose sighed in resignation.

"Gabby said something extra to me on my birthday. When you were in the bathroom. She asked me if I would listen to her."

"She did?"

"Really. She really did."

"What'd you say back?"

"Nothing. That's why I put her in the closet. I didn't want to hear her say anything else."

"That is weird."

"See? I told you."

"*Wow!*" That settled it. Now Rose knew for sure. What they had hold of was something magic. Finally, after all those years of searching and expecting, she had found it. Rose had broken wishbones, tried out wands, and gone to magicians' shows where they let you come up afterward and watch up close. Nothing worked. She had looked for circles of toadstools in the morning dew but never found anything except one large, brown mushroom in the shape of an elephant's ear. It had sprung up near the basement after a three-day rainstorm. She had reached the age when she was on the brink of giving up.

"This isn't weird after all," Rose explained now. "It isn't weird—it's magic. That's entirely different. This doll talks by herself, and she says real things."

"I was wondering," said Lucy, who wasn't sure whether a magic doll was a usual or an unusual thing.

Rose remembered the odd noise she had heard when she had first put the batteries into the doll's voice box. It had sounded like someone taking a deep breath.

Just then Mrs. Wilson came out the back door and called across the yard to them, "Do you children want to go swimming? Anita's going over to the Y with Charlie and Megan, and she says you're welcome if you want to go with them. But it's only a suggestion."

Whenever their mother said something was "only a suggestion," that meant they had to do it.

"Well, okay," Rose yelled. She reached for Gabriella.

DRIPPING BLOOD, said the doll.

Rose thought she couldn't possibly have heard right. "What did you say?" she asked. All the doll did was hiccup.

The children went indoors to get their bathing suits. Lucy left Gabriella resting on a pillow on her bed. As they started out the door, the telephone began to ring. Their mother waved them good-by as she picked up the receiver.

The Russells had air conditioning in their car, but it wasn't working that day. Even with all the windows open, it was a hot ride. Charlie sat next to one of the doors and leaned out the open window so that his mother scolded him. Now and then he turned around to be condescending to Rose and Lucy. Charlie definitely disliked girls, and he didn't keep it to himself, even when he was outnumbered. He was almost exactly Rose's age. When they had been very young, their mothers had given a joint birthday party for them. Rose could still remember it, though she had been only four. Charlie had had to be the center of attention the entire time. He went around pushing Rose and Rose's friends down, splashing water on them from the wading pool, and crying when he saw that Rose had a birthday cake too. He had had such a tantrum when Rose blew her candles out first that they'd all had to be lighted again so he could have another chance. "He's always been so competitive," his mother had said proudly.

Megan was two years younger than Charlie, but Rose thought she was mean enough to stand up to anybody. She bragged all the time. She bragged about gymnastics, she bragged about skiing, she bragged about diving, she bragged about her clothes. When they had all squeezed into the back seat and fastened their seat belts, the first thing Megan did was to pluck her special cute little swim bag out of the wayback and say, "Want to see my new bathing suit? That makes three. I've got three bathing suits. How many do you guys have?"

"Just one. We have to share it," Rose said in a sarcastic voice.

"I need a special one for racing and another one for diving. That way one can get dry in-between times. I might make the swimming team at school next year."

Rose was determined not to say anything back, but Lucy asked, "Do you have a swimming pool at your school?" with eyes as wide as two big *O*s. She was too young not to fall for Megan's traps.

"Sure we do. Don't you?"

Lucy shook her head and hung on to her towel.

"Are you old enough for school, Lucy?" Megan's voice squeaked up as if she were talking to a two-year-old.

Lucy shook her head again.

"She's going in the fall, aren't you, Luce," Rose put in.

Lucy nodded.

"Do you have a swimming pool yet?" Megan asked Rose.

"No, we don't have a swimming pool," Rose said in a voice that could have fried an egg.

"Well, excuse me! Sorry to have mentioned it!" Megan said. "We have a pool. They built it last year. It's really great. All the kids can swim, so it's really fair, you know? Nobody gets left out. It's too bad you don't go to our school."

By now Rose was grinding her teeth like a sawmill,

but she knew it wasn't much farther to the Y. Megan was never as bad in larger spaces as she was up close.

"We're going to the island pretty soon. Are you guys going back this year? We're going for an entire month, and I just can't wait to get—"

"Megan, that's enough," her mother interrupted. "Remember what I told you?"

Finally they turned into the Y parking lot.

The dressing room smelled like boiling broccoli, which made Rose and Lucy hurry into their suits all the faster. They shoved their clothes into the rusty lockers and dashed out and into the water. Megan went straight to the diving board and dived in without even wetting a toe first. Lucy was still scared of the water, so Rose stayed with her to help her get in. It was funny how Rose never felt like fighting with Lucy when the Russells were around. She suddenly turned into the perfect older sister. Charlie went off alone, throwing himself into the water with his arms barely out in front of his head. Once he was in the pool he kept ploughing up and down the training lane, swimming messily but fast. Megan didn't do anything except practice diving. "Look at me!" she would call to Rose or Lucy or anybody else near her, and *splash!* in she would go, straight and clean. Rose had to admit that Megan was a good diver. Rose couldn't dive at all, but she didn't want Megan to point this out. She decided to stay and help Lucy down at the shallow end.

And then the thing happened. Charlie came running around one corner of the pool by the deep end, slipped on some water, and fell so hard he cracked his head open on the rim of the pool. Rose could actually hear it when his head hit the tiles. He lay without moving for several seconds. Anita dropped her magazine and came scrambling around from her bench. Rose jumped up the ladder nearest her. The lifeguard climbed down from his platform in a flash. Megan had been somewhere in mid-swandive and missed Charlie's accident.

Just as everyone got near him, Charlie moved a little. He clutched his head and howled, a long screaming *ow-ow* that echoed horribly off the tile walls and low ceiling. When Rose got to him, she could see a big gash across the side of his forehead, right above his eye. Blood was dripping down from between the fingers he had clenched to his head. It formed a small pool and then ran into a puddle of water, where it swirled and sank in blurring red threads. Everyone was saying "Good Lord" and running around for towels. The lifeguard and Anita together got Charlie to his feet and helped him hold a towel across his head. They walked him between them to Anita's car, Megan, Lucy, and Rose following in a horrified little band. Charlie looked greenish white, and he was shaky in the knees. He said absolutely nothing.

"You three wait by the desk until I come back," Anita told them when they reached the car. "I'll take him straight to Emergency." Lucy and Megan and Rose went back into the Y and found their towels by the pool. They wrapped them around their shoulders and sat down to wait on the front bench. It felt as if Anita was gone to the hospital for about three hours, but, in fact, she came back to get them in forty-five minutes.

"All stitched up, and we didn't even have to wait," she said to the clerk at the desk. "Okay, kids, let's go."

The three girls got their clothes out of the lockers and climbed into the back seat of the car. Charlie sat in front, wearing a square white patch over his cut. He was already starting to sound like his usual self.

"What are you staring at?" he said with a sassy grin, as if they saw big white bandages on him every day.

"You shouldn't have run, Charlie," said Megan.

"Megan, what do you know?" he said.

"What was it like getting sewed up?" Rose asked.

"You don't feel a thing," he said.

Anita let Lucy and Rose off in front of their house. "Sorry I can't say hello to your mom," she apologized. "You tell her what happened. She should be glad she has only daughters!"

They went in the back door and straight upstairs to take off their bathing suits. As soon as she saw the doll resting stiffly against Lucy's pillow, Rose remembered. DRIPPING BLOOD, the doll had said. Suddenly the plastic baby's face didn't look like a lifeless doll face anymore. It looked knowing.

But Rose forgot that the moment she stepped into the kitchen and saw the look on her mother's face. Something terrible had happened.

CHAPTER 4

"Mom?" said Rose. "What's the matter?" In an instant her heart was pounding like a fist against the inside of her chest. Her mother's face was blotched and red, and her eyes were full of tears.

"It's Grandma Foley," she said. "Just as you left, I got a phone call. She's had a stroke, and she's very, very sick. I'm going to fly out to Iowa today, as soon as I can get my ticket."

"What's a stroke?" asked Rose. "She won't die, will she?"

"Oh, no! Grandma!" cried Lucy.

"We don't know if she will die. We hope not," said their mother firmly.

"What's a stroke?" Rose repeated.

"Grandma's stroke!" Lucy burst into tears. Mrs. Wilson picked Lucy up and sat down and hugged her on her lap. Rose slid into the chair next to them.

"A stroke is when a blood vessel in a person's brain breaks and makes some part of the brain stop working. Sometimes there are lots of bad effects, sometimes only a few."

"What's Grandma's like?" asked Rose.

"I don't know. I've been trying to reach her doctor. That was her next-door neighbor who called me. She's still alive, though, Mrs. McGurney said. She's in the hospital. It only happened this morning." Mrs. Wilson blew her nose, and Rose saw her eyes fill with tears again.

"Oh, Mom," said Rose in a soft voice. "She has to be all right. She has to."

"She does, doesn't she?" said her mother with a forced smile. "Now, you two will have to get your own lunches while I make some more phone calls." She got up and went to the telephone in the next room.

"Let's have tuna fish," Rose said to Lucy.

"I want bologna," said Lucy.

"This is no time to fight," said Rose. She got a can of tuna fish from the pantry, managed to open it, though the can opener was stiff and kept slipping off the edge, and dumped the contents of the can into a dish. She had forgotten to drain off the extra water, she realized. The tuna fish looked awfully wet. Well, never mind. She searched the refrigerator and found the jar of mayonnaise behind a dish of leftover noodles.

"I hate mayonnaise!" said Lucy, watching a giant spoonful being lifted toward the dish.

"There's always mayonnaise in tuna fish," Rose said, and plopped the spoonful in. Then, seeing Lucy was about to scream, she thought twice and scooped a little bit back out: "Look, Lucy, I took some out again."

"I want to cut celery," said Lucy.

"Mom!" Rose called. "Is Lucy old enough to cut with a knife?"

Her mother, the phone pressed to her ear, waved off Rose's question. She turned her back, talking into the receiver—"When does it leave Chicago?"—and shut the dining room door.

Well. Rose fished a bundle of celery out of the vegetable drawer and broke off one stalk. She put it on the cutting board and got out a table knife. Lucy certainly couldn't hurt herself on that.

"Here, Luce," she said, dragging a chair over to the counter. Lucy climbed up on the chair and sawed the stalk of celery into five large chunks. They were too big; but so what. Rose stirred them in.

"Did you wash the celery?" asked Mrs. Wilson, coming into the kitchen. As soon as she asked the question, Rose saw streaks of dirt in the bunch of celery that was left on the counter. Fortunately, she didn't have to answer.

"You children may have to fend for yourselves for a while," Mrs. Wilson said. "I know you're old enough and independent enough to get along when your father's here. But I'm trying to make an arrangement for you for the daytime. I can't leave you entirely alone."

This was the first time the idea came through to Rose that they were going to be without their mother. Entirely alone, did she say?

"What I'd like to do is arrange to have you and Lucy go over to the Russells' every day," she went on. "I know Anita would absolutely love to have you, and she'd take you everywhere with her two kids."

"Mom! No!" Rose squawked.

"Well, for heaven's sake, why not?"

"Well, I mean . . . Charlie hurt himself today. Bad." Rose remembered again the doll's voice warning them— DRIPPING BLOOD. And she could almost hear its voice saying something else earlier that morning. Hadn't it said MOTHER'S LEAVING?

"Oh, Charlie's always hurting himself," her mother was saying. "He's just that kind of boy."

"It isn't that. Mom, please, NO. We can't stand them, can we, Lucy? Really we can't. And we want to stay around our own house, don't we, Lucy?"

"We want to play with my doll," said Lucy.

Rose bit her lip. She had been hoping Lucy wouldn't mention the doll.

"I'm surprised to hear you say that. But I hate to make you go somewhere you really don't want to go. Still, you need to have someone around."

"How about Mrs. Donahue?" Rose suggested.

"She has a new job now, taking care of an elderly man in her apartment building."

"We could try staying by ourselves," said Rose.

"I'd worry about you too much. And you wouldn't like it. I'll be gone at least ten days or two weeks. Maybe longer."

Two weeks? Rose had been thinking it would be a few days. Two weeks was a long time. The house already began to feel empty.

"I have to think of something," Mrs. Wilson said. "And I have to hurry. My plane leaves at 8:15 tonight. Both the Smiths work, I can't ask them. So it'll have to be the Russells, unless you can come up with someone else.

This isn't like the old days when a neighborhood was full of families you could count on."

Rose made her brain whir through the possibilities. They hadn't had a baby-sitter for several months, because their parents hadn't gone out. Was there anyone they used to have? *Think*, she told herself. And sure enough, Rose's brain did as it was told, which sometimes happened. Cindy, James's afternoon baby-sitter! Rose was sure Cindy was in college. That ought to be old enough.

"I know!" she said. "James Handry has a baby-sitter. Cindy McGuire. She comes every afternoon when he gets home from camp. Try her. She's nice, Mom, I'm sure she's nice."

"Well, that's an idea," said Mrs. Wilson. "I'd rather not ask someone for such a big favor. I've seen Cindy walking to James's house. She looks like a nice girl. I wonder how I could get in touch with her, though, and with James's mother. Let me think. The Smiths probably know where Linda works. I'll get the number from them. I just hope I can reach her. Maybe the baby-sitter wouldn't mind bringing James here every day. You children could play together."

Bring James here? *Play* together? James didn't play anymore, Rose was sure of that. She started to protest, but stopped herself. If she wasn't careful, they would end up with Charlie and Megan. "Okay," she said.

Her mother turned back to the telephone, and Rose and Lucy made their sandwiches.

By midafternoon Mrs. Wilson had made the new arrangements. Mrs. Wilson whispered to Rose that she didn't like turning to someone she scarcely knew, but she was stuck this time. Linda Handry—who told her that she was about to be Linda Donaldson again, now that the divorce was final—said it was just fine with her; it would be good for James to have other kids to play with. Then Mrs. Wilson telephoned Cindy, who said it was a great idea, that she'd really like the extra money, and she would start tomorrow. She could get there before Mr. Wilson left in the morning, and James would come over to the Wilsons' when he got home from camp. The four of them would stay mostly at the Wilsons', but they would go up to James's house if they wanted to or if Linda needed them to. So it was all set with Cindy and the grown-ups, and everyone said what a great thing it was going to be. Rose and Lucy didn't say anything. They weren't so sure how great it was going to be, but it could have been so much worse.

Then Mrs. Wilson called Anita Russell and asked her to stop in now and then to check on things. Anita promptly offered to take Rose and Lucy every afternoon. Mrs. Wilson said no thanks, that was much too much to ask; the girls would be perfectly fine here, but perhaps once in a while they could go for a swim with the Russells. Rose made a face at Lucy when she heard this. Mrs. Wilson packed her suitcase, and Mr. Wilson came home from the office early. They all drove to the airport.

"Mom, what do you think is going to happen to Grandma?" asked Rose as they wove in and out of heavy traffic. It was hard to imagine Grandma Foley lying in a hospital bed, probably with tubes in her arms, unconscious all day long, and wearing one of those sad hospital nightgowns that they always made you wear. Grandma

Foley was Rose and Lucy's only grandmother. She said she intended to spoil her granddaughters, and she enjoyed doing it. Rose's mother said Grandma had never been that way when she was growing up. She could hardly believe how unfussy Grandma was about things her grandchildren did, compared with the way she had been in the old days. Rose thought her mother sounded annoyed about this. Grandma Foley would just laugh and say, "You'll be this way, too, when you're a grandmother." "Well, I hope so!" Rose's mother would say in an exasperated tone. Grandma Foley sent Rose trinkets and junk toys, always just the one that Rose was interested in at the moment. She had sent Barbie-doll clothes, and then Cabbage-Patch-kid clothes. Once she had sent a digital watch in the shape of a crayon box; other times it was jewelry or play makeup. There weren't going to be any UPS packages from Far Corners, Iowa, for a long time now, though, not until she got better. She had to get better.

"I just don't know, nobody knows," her mother was replying. "That's one thing that's difficult about this, we don't know what will happen. But I'll call you as soon as I find out anything. Your grandma would love to hear from you as soon as she's well enough to read again. So I want both you children to write her some get-well letters. Just send them to her house. Daddy has the address in the address book. I'll be staying there and I'll take her mail to her."

"We will," promised Lucy solemnly.

Rose didn't say anything. Her stomach had suddenly clutched, and she wondered if she was going to throw up. She hated saying good-by.

Mr. Wilson parked the car, and they sat inside the airport terminal nervously waiting in plastic chairs. Music was being piped in, and the sound made Rose's stomach even more uncertain. At last the roomful of waiting passengers sprang to their feet and surged toward the exit. Their father kissed their mother, and then she kissed and hugged Rose and Lucy. She hurried down the corridor after the other passengers and was quickly lost to sight.

That was it. For how long?

The car was empty and dark with just three of them riding home.

"Daddy, Mom won't be gone long, will she?" asked Rose.

"Goodness, I don't think so," said her father. "I'm sure Grandma will be back on her feet in no time."

Something in the tone of his voice made Rose doubt it, made her doubt it very much.

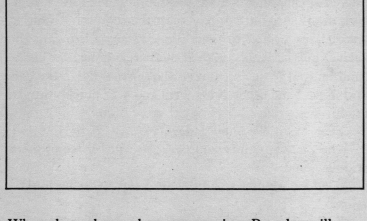

CHAPTER 5

When she woke up the next morning, Rose lay still, not wanting to wake Lucy yet. The house seemed extremely empty, as though many people had left, not just one. No sounds of breakfast came up from the kitchen: no clink of china, no footsteps, no hum of the refrigerator as its door was opened, no faint whistle of the teakettle. Instead—nothing. The emptiness of the house gave Rose an empty feeling herself, almost as if things weren't real anymore. She sat up and looked out her window at the street and sidewalk below. The paper boy on his bicycle, a dog stopping beside a tree, two joggers in gray shorts, a line of cars waiting for the green light: They looked far away and toylike, a Christmas scene behind a glass storefront, only it wasn't winter. Everything was quiet and still, except for a thread of music coming from Mr. Edgar's apartment. He must be playing his record again. Rose felt the faintest tingle of excitement. With her mother gone, they could spend all day with the doll.

Where was Gabby now?

Rose looked over at Lucy's bed.

Where was Lucy?

Rose scrambled out of bed and looked quickly around the room. Nothing. She ran over to Lucy's window and peered out. Her sister, still in her nightgown, was on the driveway far below, tucking a pink bundle into her doll stroller. She turned and began pushing it down the driveway. In another minute she came back up the driveway, followed by Cindy. Rose was down the stairs in an instant.

"Hi, guys," said Cindy, as she stepped in the back door. "Sleeping in, are you? Hi, Mr. Wilson."

Their father, dressed for work, appeared in the kitchen. " 'Morning, Cindy. Glad to see you're on time. I didn't wake the girls, because I thought you might get their breakfast. They can show you where everything is. I've also tried to make up a grocery list. I'll be doing the cooking, of course. I hope you don't mind a quick trip up to the corner market for a few things. Mrs. Wilson and I really appreciate this, you know. We're in quite a spot."

"It's okay, Mr. Wilson. They're good kids, aren't you? I haven't got anything else to do." Cindy smiled at Rose and Lucy and at Mr. Wilson. She wore a retainer on her top teeth, but except for that, Rose thought she was just about perfect. She had long, long, straight blond hair and wore tight short-shorts and painted her nails, which also were long. Today she was wearing turquoise studs in her pierced ears, and she had on turquoise jellies and a plastic turquoise belt. "You don't have to worry about a thing," Cindy went on.

Gabby, still wrapped tightly in a pink cotton doll blanket, hadn't said anything yet, maybe because Lucy was holding her upside down.

"Now you chicks be good," their father said, stooping to kiss them. "My phone number's on the refrigerator, in case you need to reach me. Let me know if your mother calls. And remember—don't talk to any strangers!"

"Well, then," said Cindy, as he left to catch his bus. "How about some breakfast. Where's the cereal?"

"Can I have a scrambled egg?" asked Lucy. She turned the blanketed bundle right side up and looked into its face. "Hey, little cutie, still asleep, huh?" she said to it. It didn't speak.

"It's way too hot for eggs," said Cindy. "How about Cheerios? What's your mom got up here? No sugar stuff, huh?" Cindy opened the cabinets and surveyed their contents. "Here we go." She got down two bowls, poured out Cheerios, and put the bowls on the table. "Cute dishes," she said.

"Our mom usually puts little plates under the bowls," said Lucy.

"You want a little plate?" asked Cindy. She got down two little plates and handed them to Rose. "Why don't you put these on the table?" she said. Then she turned on the television set and flicked the dial to a program that showed a roomful of women in leotards bending and stretching. "No color, huh?" she said.

"Nope, we only got black-and-white," said Lucy. She unwrapped Gabriella and propped her in an empty chair.

"Hi-ya!" said the doll.

"What's your dolly's name?" asked Cindy. She kicked off her jellies and did a couple of quick sideways bends by the stove in time with the women on television.

"Gabby."

"Gabby? She's a talker, huh?"

"Yep. She *really* talks," said Lucy.

"What's she say?" Cindy touched her toes, saying something like "whump."

"All kinds of stuff. She can talk by herself."

"It's only her batteries," Rose interrupted, trying to catch Lucy's eye.

"Oh yeah? Good for her." Cindy studied the position of the instructor, who was smiling constantly and exhorting her class to "come on, come on, really move it." Cindy bounced heavily from one foot to the other, lifting her knees up high.

"Well, you're kind of quiet, there," she said to Rose, stopping to catch her breath. "Are you missing your mom? You'll feel better in a while. You'll go outside after breakfast and forget about your mom being away."

"It isn't that," Rose started to say—but then for a moment it was that.

"You're a big girl," Cindy went on, resuming her hopping from foot to foot. "Now you two finish up your cereal."

Rose ate her cereal quickly, though it tasted terrible; Lucy left most of hers.

"Ma-ma!" said Gabriella. Uh-oh, thought Rose. Maybe she was getting warmed up.

"Hi-ya!" said Gabriella.

"Well, hi-ya to you, too!" Cindy answered with a laugh.

"Hey, we better brush our teeth now!" Rose announced, jumping up. She snatched Gabriella off the chair and tucked her under her arm. "Our mom always makes us brush our teeth right after breakfast," she said. "Come on, Luce." She ran up the back stairs to their room. In a moment Lucy followed her up. Rose went into the bathroom and turned on the water faucet full blast to cover up the sound of her voice.

"Lucy, we can't tell anybody about Gabriella," she said.

"Mom doesn't always make us brush our teeth right after breakfast," said Lucy.

"I know. But I needed to tell you something and get Gabby out of there. We've got to keep her a secret from everybody, even from Cindy. Even from Dad and Mom. Till we get her figured out." It was hard to tell when Lucy would talk about something and when she would be quiet. "This is really important. This is the most important thing we've ever not told."

"Mm-hmm." Lucy hummed a vague agreement between her foamy teeth.

"Promise you won't tell?"

"Okay."

"Promise out loud."

"*I promise I won't tell.* But why?"

"Because we want to know what she does. If you tell about magic things, they can stop working."

"Right." It was too complicated for Lucy to follow, and it didn't seem important. Lucy didn't particularly care who knew about Gabby and who didn't. But if Rose said not to tell, she would try not to. Lucy just wanted to play with Gabby. She wanted to put doll clothes on her and take them off her and push her in the doll stroller.

Rose had been planning to take Gabby off to the farthest corner of the yard, but when she and Lucy had finished brushing their teeth and making their beds—just for good measure, to impress Cindy all the more that they were good and didn't need looking after—the doorbell rang. It was Anita, already stopping by to see that everything was all right. Rose persuaded Lucy to leave Gabriella upstairs, to be on the safe side. After Anita drove off, Cindy decided they needed to go for a walk around the pond. They crossed the parkway and ambled across the grass to the asphalt path that circled the pond. They stopped and watched bicyclists and dogs and little sailboats and rowboats. Cindy knew the fellow who was in charge of renting the boats, and she went over to the dock and talked to him for a long time. They didn't talk about boats. "That was Ron," she said to Rose and Lucy when they started home. She shook her earrings and turned faintly pink.

After that it was lunchtime, and after lunch Cindy had them walk up the street with her to the corner, where a man had opened a vegetable stand in an old gas station. Mrs. Wilson would never go to the vegetable stand, because the man didn't refrigerate anything. Cindy bought carrots, lettuce, green grapes, plums, and some strawberries that looked a little old but smelled wonderful.

Rose still didn't want to bring Gabriella downstairs till they could be sure no one was watching or listening.

Lucy was getting impatient. "She's my new doll and I want to play with her!" she complained to Rose crossly. Cindy was putting the vegetables into the refrigerator.

"Sshh!" said Rose. "Just wait a while, okay?"

"What's the problem?" asked Cindy.

"We were going to play a game with the talking doll," lied Rose. "But her batteries have to rest first. Lucy keeps forgetting. Otherwise the batteries will wear out in one day."

"We can always get more," said Cindy. "They've got them at the drugstore."

"That's right, I forgot," Rose said, and the subject was dropped.

James trudged up the sidewalk at three-thirty. He rang the back doorbell, then stepped in before anyone could answer it. He stood on one side of the kitchen, and Rose and Lucy stood on the other side, behind the kitchen counter. His face was pink from the heat, and Rose could see pale orange freckles all over his face and arms. He was sweating, and he looked very tough.

"I've got water on my ear," he said to Cindy, ignoring Lucy and Rose. "They make us swim twice a day, *with* instructors, whether we want to or not."

"It's probably good for you," said Cindy.

"It's not good for us," James said.

"How's the diving going?"

"Terrible."

"Well, how about the soccer?"

"It's all right. It's too hot for that stuff. Say, have you got any soda?" He looked in Rose and Lucy's direction, but not really at them.

"Our mom doesn't get us soda. But we've got lemonade," said Rose.

"That'll be okay," said James.

Cindy opened a package of Oreos and James immediately ate five in a row. She got out the pitcher of lemonade and poured glasses for all of them. James gulped his down and poured another.

"So I'm supposed to stay here all afternoon?" he asked.

"You three can go outside and play," said Cindy.

"Go . . . out . . . side . . . and . . . play?" he said, separating each syllable, as if Cindy had told him to eat worms. "Why can't I just go home?"

"Your mother doesn't want you there by yourself all afternoon," said Cindy.

"I don't need a baby-sitter," James said. "You can stay here with these kids and I'll go home."

"Not today, James. Your mother would kill me."

James shrugged his shoulders in disgust.

"Well, we didn't ask for you to come here, so don't blame us," Rose blurted out. As soon as she said it, she realized it wasn't true.

James appeared to be considering this. "So what's there to do around here? Have you got any games?"

"We've got Sorry and Backgammon and Trivial Pursuit," said Rose.

"I guess I don't feel like playing games," James said.

"I'm going outside," said Rose. "You can come out or stay in. I could care less!" She walked out of the kitchen, slamming the door, and stalked over through the weeds to the stone bench under the cherry tree and sat down. In a few moments she heard another slam of the back door, and Lucy came threading her way through the weeds to the bench, too.

"Uh-oh!" said a high little voice.

"Oh, no, Lucy! Why did you bring her here?" cried Rose.

A third slam of the back door, and James was coming out toward the stone bench, too. "You got some kind of secret hiding place out here?" he asked, sounding less insulting than before.

The doll hiccupped.

"What was that?" said James.

"Just Lucy's doll," Rose answered, hoping she sounded bored.

"A hiccupping doll? Does it burp, too?" James hooted with laughter.

"Uh-oh," said Gabriella again. BLOOD WILL FLOW.

Rose and Lucy froze.

"What was that? What did it say?" asked James. "Hey, can I see it?"

"No! You can't!" said Rose.

"But it's not even yours," James said to her.

BLOOD, repeated Gabriella.

"What's it saying?" James reached for the doll.

"Don't let him have it! You absolutely can*not* have it!" Rose yelled. It was too late. The urgency in her voice had made the doll irresistible. James yanked it out of Lucy's arms and ran crashing through the bushes and weeds in maddening circles, hollering "Ha, ha, your baby has the hiccups!" Rose and Lucy chased after him, shrieking. James stopped abruptly and Rose ran right into him. The doll flew out of his hands like a football and landed with a thump on the grass—a thump that evoked a series of squeaks and painful whines from the voice box. James darted over and snatched it back up.

"In case you didn't know, that doll happens to be a particularly special doll!" Rose shouted, standing stock-still with her fists on her hips. "If you break it, you are responsible—for whatever happens. That doll has magic powers. If you wreck them, you're responsible. So give it here. And don't drop it again. You may have already ruined it!" Tears of frustration made her voice high and squeaky. Lucy joined in the screaming.

"Oh, brother. Can't you take a joke?" James handed the doll back to Lucy.

"It's not a joke," said Rose.

"So it's so special? It has these magic powers? What powers?"

"Well, I . . ." Rose didn't want to tell him, or anyone.

"Girls. They're all hysterical," James said in disgust.

"All right. I'll tell you. She talks. By herself. She has this voice box that cries and says the usual stuff like 'Mama.' But then sometimes the voice box says other things. Like just now, when she said BLOOD WILL FLOW. She doesn't usually say that. And there's something else. Sometimes she says something, and then awhile later a thing happens. It's as if the idea for what happens comes from the doll."

"Like what? What are you talking about?"

"Well, we have these friends, the Russells—well, they aren't exactly our friends, but our mom makes us go swimming with them at the Y sometimes. So the other day, before we went, the doll said DRIPPING BLOOD. She was out here under the cherry tree, and that's what she said. Then we went swimming, and one of our friends fell and cut his head open. Sure enough, there was all this dripping blood."

"You're putting me on."

"No." Rose shook her head.

"It could have been just a coincidence."

"Just a coincidence? A doll says DRIPPING BLOOD and you think it's a coincidence?"

"Hmm," said James.

"We're going to try to figure out what makes her say the things. You can help us. But if you tell anybody, anybody at all, you'll be sorry. Really sorry. The sorriest you've ever been."

"I won't tell. I swear."

"What do you swear on? How do we know?" Rose pressed him.

"I'll swear on the Bible. If you've got one."

They had one, but Rose wasn't sure where it was. "We'll do that later," she said. "Now let's get completely out of sight."

They pushed their way back of the cherry tree into a green thicket, going slowly and casually, so that it wouldn't look as if they were up to anything. That way, even if they were seen, no one would pay any attention to them. And almost no one did. Only one pair of eyes watched the children disappear under the bush.

CHAPTER · 6

"It's prickly under here," James complained. Rose was the first to stoop down and slip under the overhanging branches, and she accidentally let a few snap back at him.

"It's better in the middle," she said over her shoulder. With a few more grunts and groans, they reached the center of the green cave. The light filtered through the green leaves, so even the air had a green color. There was just room for the three of them to sit in a semicircle.

Rose turned the painted stool right side up and set Gabriella down on it. The stool fell over. She righted it, wiggling it back and forth and pushing its three legs firmly down through the leaves and into the dirt. The haunting fragrance released by the crushed leaves was in the air. She set Gabriella on the seat, now firmly fixed, and propped her gently forward. The voice box whirred, as it always did, but this was followed by a silence rather than the usual words.

"What now?" said James.

"Beats me," said Rose. She tilted Gabriella from side to side. She shook her. They heard clicking and whirring, but no words. Rose replaced her on the stool.

"We're listening, so why don't you say something?" said Lucy.

"Sshh, we can't talk to her like she was somebody's baby brother," said Rose.

"What is *that?* Look out!" James shouted. He spread his arms, as if to push Rose and Lucy back out of harm's way, and jumped up. When Rose saw what he was staring at, she scrambled to a crouching position and grabbed Lucy up from the leafy floor. A large, repulsive black snake moved toward them, sliding under the stool, its flat head outthrust in unmistakable hostility. They tried to back up, but the snake slid after them, coming right up to their feet. It seemed to be trying to chase them away.

"Get out of here!" screamed Rose. She thrashed backward through the branches, pulling Lucy after her.

"Kill it!" James cried.

"It's coming after us!"

"It's going to get me!"

"Kill it!"

"Run for your life!"

James tore his way through the bushes and looked desperately around. He caught sight of an old snow shovel lying beside the garage, and he raced over and grabbed it up. Its blade was twisted, bent, and rusty, but it was heavy. James ran back to the snake. He lifted the shovel high over his head and brought it down with tremendous force on the snake's body, right behind its head. He hadn't known he was so strong.

"Don't look," he said as he lifted the shovel. The snake writhed feebly, thrashed its tail, and lay still, its head cut from its body.

Rose and Lucy rushed over.

"It's sickening!" said Lucy.

Yet in some strange way, it was not. The snake scarcely seemed real, so quickly had life left its body. A dark fluid pooled on the surface of the ground beside it.

"Is that its blood?" asked Rose.

"Doesn't look like real blood," said James. The fluid soaked quickly into the ground. It had a terrible smell, like burning rubber. "Phew! I don't know *what* it can be!"

He looked down at the shovel, but its blade was perfectly clean.

The three children looked at one another. From within the bush came some clicking sounds. "Maybe we ought to go back in," said Rose.

They crawled cautiously back into the cave. "She's still here," said Lucy, "right on her chair."

Rose sat down cross-legged in front of the doll. She had the distinct sense that a knowing presence inhabited the doll's painted face. "Do you have anything to say to us?" she asked in a whisper. "We're listening, if you do."

I AM YOURS, said the doll.

James pressed his lips together. "What'd I tell you?" whispered Rose.

"But she's already mine!" said Lucy.

"I don't think that's what she means," whispered Rose.

ASK . . . ASK, said the doll.

"Ask what? What should we ask?" said Rose. It felt awkward talking to a toy.

There was a rattling noise, and the pebbles in the bowl jiggled around, as if someone had jostled the bowl. Then the doll replied: THE SERPENT IS DEAD. THE SPIRIT OF PROPHECY SPEAKS ONCE MORE.

That did it. All three children turned and ran.

CHAPTER · 7

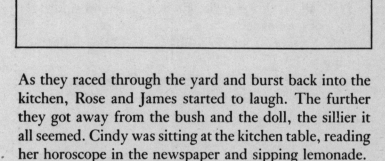

As they raced through the yard and burst back into the kitchen, Rose and James started to laugh. The further they got away from the bush and the doll, the sillier it all seemed. Cindy was sitting at the kitchen table, reading her horoscope in the newspaper and sipping lemonade.

"What's the story?" she asked as they came running and jostling in.

"Oh, nothing, we're just fooling around," said James.

"You can do that outside," Cindy said.

"I know. We were," said James. He and Rose began to laugh wildly. Lucy started to cry.

"They weren't teasing you, were they, honey?" asked Cindy.

"No. But the doll is talking too much," said Lucy.

"Well, you just stop listening to it," said Cindy.

"And there was a scary snake out there. But James killed it."

"James did what?"

"There was a snake that was chasing after us, and James chopped its head off," said Lucy.

There was no stopping Lucy once she started telling things.

"It was just a plain old garden snake," said James, fibbing easily. "And I went *thwack*, just like that!" He brought down an imaginary blade, and he and Rose went off into gales of hysterical laughter.

"Ugh!" Cindy shivered. "Well, have some lemonade."

They all sat down at the kitchen table and sipped tall glasses of lemonade.

"Did you bring in the doll?" asked Rose suddenly, turning to Lucy.

"No. And I'm *not* going out there to get her."

Rose didn't like the idea much herself. "We'll get her later, when Dad gets home," she said.

"After supper we'll call your mother," said Mr. Wilson. He stood by the stove in a large blue apron, pouring a package of Spanish-rice mix into a pot of boiling water.

"We don't like Spanish rice, Dad," said Rose.

"Oh, no?" said Mr. Wilson. He put a lid on the pot. "Try just a taste. Maybe you'll start to like it." He busied himself collecting the ingredients for a salad from various corners of the refrigerator: lettuce, a tomato, a cucumber, a purple onion. Rose's father had cooked their supper other times, too. He usually gave them helpings that were way too big, but he was good at cooking their favorites: cheeseburgers (he made them with the right kind of cheese), corn on the cob, and spaghetti with meatballs.

He had his own recipe for spaghetti sauce, made from scratch, and he made meatballs from his own special recipe, too.

Tonight they were having cheeseburgers. Rose opened the package of American cheese and peeled off four slices. That was one too many. She had forgotten. A twist of lonesomeness curdled her stomach.

"There was an awful snake in the backyard today, Dad," she said. She half hoped her father would ask her lots of questions about it, the way her mother would if she were there. "You should go out and look at it. James killed it. It came after us."

"It came after you? I've never heard of a snake doing that. Most garden snakes are afraid of human beings." The hamburgers began to sizzle in the big black frying pan. Mr. Wilson gave the pan a little shake.

"It didn't look like a garden snake."

"We'll take a look at it after supper. You say James killed it? That's too bad."

"He had to."

"Was it a garter snake? Garter snakes are good for a garden, you know. They help keep out pests."

"It wasn't a garter snake." Rose remembered the moment of terror when the snake had suddenly appeared and she couldn't get away from it.

"Now let's see. I forgot to set the timer for the Spanish rice."

"We don't like Spanish rice," said Lucy.

"So I hear," their father said in a good-natured voice. "It's lucky that it's one of my favorites!"

"Dad," said Rose.

"Yes, Rose?"

"Dad . . . do you believe in magic? Sshh, Lucy, don't interrupt!"

"To be truthful, no, I don't."

"But do you know for sure that there isn't any?"

"Let's put it this way. If someone proved to me that magic existed, I would be very surprised."

"Did you believe in magic when you were little?"

"It's hard to remember," said Mr. Wilson. "That was such a long time ago. Why? Do you?"

"Oh, I don't know. Sometimes, maybe. I was just wondering. And . . . Dad?"

"Yes, Rose."

"What's prophecy?"

"Prophecy?"

"Yes."

"Prophecy means 'prediction of the future.' Sometimes it is used to mean predictions that supposedly came from God, or a god. We don't believe in prophecy these days. But in ancient times people did. The Greeks and Romans believed in prophecy. Have you been reading something about it?"

"No, not exactly. Just something I heard. I was just wondering."

"Now, who wants a toasted roll for her cheeseburger?"

"Me!" cried Lucy.

"Dad," said Rose. "Did prophecies come true?"

"I suppose some of them must have come true. People used to use all kinds of things to try to predict the future. Sometimes they would look for omens."

"For what-ems?"

"Omens. Those were things that happened that people would interpret as signs, as meaning something about the future. For example, if they heard a dog bark in a certain way, they might decide that meant that bad luck was coming. They attached meaning to these omens, even though—"

"Dad, the rolls are burning!" said Lucy.

"It's an omen!" said Rose.

"Well, sort of," grumbled their father, pulling a tray of blackened circles from the oven. "Good thing we have the rest of the package." He arranged three more hamburger rolls on the baking sheet and put them back in the oven.

"Now that was not really an omen. At least, I hope not. But if we had a big fire the next day, then we would all think that the burned rolls had been an omen. Then there were oracles—"

"Daddy, the rolls," said Lucy.

"I'm watching. These are going to be toasty, perfectly brown."

"So what about the oracles?"

"There were oracles in ancient Greece, for instance. Special priestesses were chosen to interpret what the oracles said. I think we're finally ready. Who wants to eat?"

"I need ketchup!" said Lucy.

"You can reach it yourself," said Mr. Wilson.

"What about the oracles?" asked Rose.

"There are many stories about the oracles, especially the Oracle of Delphi. The oracle always spoke the truth. That was the belief, anyhow. And the oracle's prophecies would come true, sometimes in surprising ways. Heavens, I haven't thought about this since I took a course in mythology in college. I didn't know I could remember so much."

"Can we start?" asked Lucy.

"The oracles were supposed to be mouthpieces for the gods. They were in special places like caves, or even trees. The gods spoke through priestesses, or through rustling leaves, or through pebbles dancing around in a bowl."

"Dad," said Rose.

"Yes, dearie."

"I'm not sure I feel like eating."

Their father dialed Grandma Foley's phone number after they had finished supper, but the line was busy. "What about this snake, then?" he said. "We'll try your mother again in a moment."

Rose and Lucy led him across the backyard to the tangle of underbrush near the green cave. There they found the small, thin body of a green snake, about as big around as a pencil.

"Hey," Rose said in dismay. "This isn't the same one. It's not the same at all." The head had been cut off, though. The snake had to be the same one. All around it were trampled weeds and the footprints they had made that afternoon. Could they have imagined that it was big and ugly? All three of them, imagining the same thing at once?

"Maybe it startled you so much that you thought it looked bigger," suggested their father.

"It isn't that one," said Lucy. "Or else it got smaller when it died."

"Let's try your mother again," said Mr. Wilson.

They kept trying to get through to Iowa, between loading the dishwasher and putting away the leftover rice, until at last their mother answered the phone. Rose could tell from what her father said that things were very serious, that the news of Grandma Foley was not good.

"Hi, dear," her mother said when Rose finally got her turn on the telephone.

"Hi, Mom."

"I'm going to be out here quite awhile, it looks like. Grandma was worse today."

"What happened?"

"She's not getting better as fast as the doctors think she should. How are you three? Your father tells me you've already cleaned up the kitchen."

"Yep. We had a pretty good time with James, Mom. And Cindy is nice."

"She doesn't let you have too many sweet things, does she?"

"No. But Mom. When are you coming back?"

"I can't say yet. You'll just have to do the best you can. I know you'll be fine."

"We're fine. But Mom. It's nicer when you're here."

"It's nicer for me, too. I miss you, Rose, and Lucy, too."

Rose wanted to drag the conversation out, but she knew she had to say good-by.

"My turn!" Lucy was already jumping up and down, trying to grab the telephone.

"Mom, do you want Lucy?"

"Sure. Now you be a help to your father."

"I will. I am." She handed the phone to Lucy. She felt worse after talking than she had felt before.

Everyone felt so miserable after their phone conversation that they sat down together and watched a perfectly awful program on television. Then Mr. Wilson made popcorn, and, even though they weren't hungry, the delicious smell and the warm, salty kernels were comforting. It wasn't until he was tucking them into bed that Rose suddenly remembered.

"Hey, we left the doll outside," she said, sitting up again after her father had given her a final neck rub.

"Now it's too late for you to go outside, Rose. Especially after dark."

"But she can't be out all night! Poor Gabby!" Lucy cried.

"I tell you what. I'll go out and get her for you. You two go to sleep, and I'll go outside and get her before I go to bed."

"Do you promise?" asked Rose.

"Yes." He kissed them both, and Rose heard the creaking of his footsteps as he went down to the kitchen. Then she heard the phone ring, and she heard him shut the kitchen door. And then she fell asleep.

Rose awoke some time later. She knew instantly that her father had forgotten to bring in the doll. She could sense it, in a thoroughly creepy way. She lay still, not wanting to move. She knew what she was going to do, but she didn't want to do it yet. She would go out to the yard herself and bring in the doll. Her parents had lectured her and lectured her about not going outside alone after dark. But she had to now—she did not want to disturb her father. And something more compelled her than just the need to bring Gabriella inside. She was beginning to feel responsible for the doll. And she wanted to see how much it would really say, when there was no one to interrupt. Wide awake now, she got out of bed, picked up her sandals, and tiptoed very slowly downstairs, making no noise at all.

The back-door key hung next to the row of coat hooks. She could picture her mother hanging it there after she had locked up at night. Rose peered out the window. The long, shadowy yard was lit by a late moon. The sky was very bright, even blue, and clouds moved across the face of the moon. Silvery white light lay over Rose's familiar territory: the brick patio, the rusty lounge chair, the overgrown rhododendrons, and beyond them the deep tangle of bushes where Gabriella was still sitting. Probably.

Once she had unlocked the door, it would seem easier. Other rings of keys jingled as she slipped the back-door key off the hook. Carefully she worked it into the lock, slowly turned it, and winced as the bolt clacked back. She waited. Her father's snoring drifted from his bedroom. She opened the door, stepped out, and closed it silently behind her. She sat down on the back steps to put on her sandals. Though she had no idea what time it was, it had to be late, way past midnight, because she couldn't hear any cars, even on the parkway.

Night sounds filled Rose's ears: summer insects and animals rustling and murmuring and calling. Out beyond the back stoop lay a midnight wilderness. She balled her fists up tightly a few times, just to convince herself that she was truly awake. The yard looked immense. The best thing was to walk as fast as she could. What danger could there be, really? Robbers would be in bed by now, and there was no such thing as a ghost or a spook or a monster. There was just a plain old talking doll. Just a plain old . . .

Now that she was walking across the yard she felt numb. Already past the garbage cans, already beyond the patch of herbs—then a creature appeared from no-where, and Rose stopped in her tracks. A dark-colored animal, its body low to the ground, its long tail flowing, strolled right toward her. The creature's pointed nose swerved smoothly from side to side. Its white stripe glowed in the moonlight. Rose let out her breath as the skunk, ignoring her, slipped under the fence and dis-appeared behind the neighbors' garbage can.

She was there now. Faintly, far within the bushes, she could see the gleam of Gabriella's white socks. Rose crouched down and pushed her way into the cave. Gabby sat exactly where they had left her, propped on the rick-ety stool. Rose glanced around her. She could hear crea-tures stirring in the leaves, but she couldn't see any of them. She heard a click and a whir and then a silence that seemed to be a listening silence. The bushes con-tained creaks, snaps, rustles, swishes; within the cave, the silence continued. *Ask, ask,* Rose thought to herself, but no words came.

WHY HAVE YOU CALLED ME? the doll asked suddenly, in a clear, rather musical voice.

Rose jumped. "Oh, my gosh! I didn't know I had!"

DO YOU WISH TO ASK SOMETHING? The voice seemed to come from far away, yet it sounded as close as her knee.

Rose's brain felt like a television that was set between stations: all static and conflicting signals. "I mean, I say, well, I guess I do have something to ask. Who are you?" She hoped she didn't sound too disrespectful. What if she made Gabby mad? She looked closer at the doll's face. Though the prim, smiling features didn't move, they seemed to have acquired a look of concentration.

There were whirring and clicking sounds, followed by a long, startling hiss, and then the clear voice spoke: I AM THE ORACLE.

"I don't know very much about oracles. Are you the only one?"

THE ONLY ORACLE, came the reply.

"And do you answer people's questions?"

I DO. I AM THE ORACLE. THE DOLL HAS GIVEN ME A VOICE.

"Oh. You mean you're *in* the doll?"

IN THE DOLL, she said, repeating Rose's words. There was another long hissing. DO YOU WISH TO ASK A QUESTION ABOUT WHAT IS TO COME?

She had to ask something about the future, didn't she? Why hadn't she thought this out? "Let me see. Er, how about the weather? What will it be like tomorrow? And, let's see. Will anything exciting happen?" She felt like an idiot. She was probably wasting the doll's powers.

ICE! A DROWNING! A definitive click followed, as if something had shut off. The spirit, or whatever it was, was gone. Rose could tell by the vacant look that had moved back into Gabriella's face.

Ice? That was the weather? And a drowning—that was what she called "exciting"?

Rose shivered. She was glad the doll had turned itself off. Right now she didn't want to hear anything else it had to say. She scooped Gabriella up in the crook of one elbow and crawled backward out of the bush. As she made her way across the yard, something caught her eye. Someone with gleaming white hair was standing on the second-floor deck. It was Mr. Edgar. He was leaning on the rail and looking right at her. He didn't say a word. Rose shifted her eyes away and walked fast, straight into the house, and pretended she had not seen him.

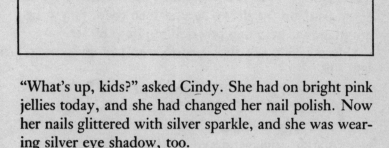

CHAPTER 8

"What's up, kids?" asked Cindy. She had on bright pink jellies today, and she had changed her nail polish. Now her nails glittered with silver sparkle, and she was wearing silver eye shadow, too.

"We'll just go outside and read," said Rose.

"Bored already, are you?" Cindy turned on the exercise program.

"I wish James got here earlier," said Rose. "Does he always have to go to camp?"

"Well, his mother paid for it. Why do you want to know? You two think you might turn into friends?"

"We might. He could come here instead of going to camp, and we could play outside or go up to Center Street, things like that."

"I don't know," said Cindy. "What would your mother say?"

"Oh, she wouldn't care. She likes us to have friends," said Rose.

"It never hurts to ask," said Cindy. "James doesn't like camp, I know that. Why don't you ask him when he gets here. Makes no difference to me." Cindy's voice was swallowed up as she lay down on her back and began bicycling her legs in the air.

The Russells showed up around ten, just as Rose was afraid they would. One thing was for sure: After what the doll said last night, she was not going near any swimming pool today. She was stretched out under the cherry tree reading, when she heard the fatal crunch and thud of sneakers on the driveway and then there they were, grinning, and standing practically on top of her.

"Mom says we're supposed to take you swimming," said Megan.

"And Lucy, too. Where's your suit?"

Rose stood up. "I don't feel like going," she said. "We don't have to go swimming." She could see Anita, waiting in her station wagon at the end of the driveway. "Besides, there's a good reason why I don't want to go. I have a feeling something awful may happen."

"Like what?"

"Like somebody getting drowned."

"Oh, baloney!" said Charlie.

"It's just a feeling I have," said Rose. "So you can tell your mom."

"Mom! She says no! She's afraid she'll get drowned!" Megan yelled across the yard.

Anita got out of her station wagon, and Cindy came out of the house, and Lucy followed, too, holding Gabby by the hair.

"Well, I'm sure the pool is perfectly safe," Anita said.

"But of course you don't have to come. I promised your mother I'd take you a few places while she's away. Maybe next time. We could go to a movie or the science museum."

"That'd be nice," said Rose in a wooden voice.

"Hi-ya!" said Gabriella.

"What a sweet little doll!" exclaimed Anita. "Is she new?"

"I got her for my birthday," said Lucy.

"Everybody wants these talking dolls this year, don't they? They're terribly popular."

"I don't like those dolls," Megan declared. "I have three dolls at home that are just like ones in the Children's Museum. We saw them on display in the glass cabinets. So my mom and I took mine to the museum and had them appraised."

"You had them praised?" Rose giggled.

"*Ap*-praised," Megan corrected Rose testily. "They have a doll expert, you know, who is in charge of their collection. He can look at your dolls and tell you whether they are valuable."

"Oh."

"He told me mine are all valuable. So we have to put them away, to keep them perfect. He told us about preserving them and how much money they might be worth someday."

"That's enough of that subject, Megan," said Anita. "The man we saw about the dolls, Mr. Edgar, lives right in Rose and Lucy's house, doesn't he, girls? Your mother once told me she was sure he was retired, but that he worked some days at the Children's Museum. I was going to tell her all about our visit to his office—but I guess it will have to wait till she comes home again. Have you had any news about your grandma?"

"Mom's supposed to call again tonight," said Rose. "Last night she said Grandma wasn't getting better."

"Oh, Rose." Anita's voice was sympathetic. Rose wondered how Anita could be so nice when her children were so awful. "Give her my best, won't you. Now, come on, kids." Anita looked at her watch. "It's getting late, and we've got to get to the pool before it gets crowded. 'Bye, Rose; 'bye, Lucy."

Things were getting more peculiar by the hour, thought Rose, and the peculiarity was getting closer and closer to home.

If she only knew Mr. Edgar, she would be able to talk to him about it. But she didn't. Their mother had always been so strict about not talking to Mr. Edgar and not bothering him. Their mother was always strict about things like that—not becoming too friendly with people who weren't in their family or who weren't just like them. Anita Russell was okay, but James's mother wasn't, quite. Well, now that her mother was gone, she didn't have to follow all those rules. The idea made her squirm, though. Was this any way to be—she could hear a scolding voice ask—just because her mother was gone and her grandmother was so sick?

What Rose really needed to do was tell James about last night. If only she could squeeze the hours together until three-thirty.

Rose was waiting on the sidewalk when James's bus came around the corner. She waved and ran over to him as he jumped off the bus.

"What are you doing here?" he asked in surprise.

"I've got some more to tell you about the doll," Rose whispered. "And I've got an idea. Maybe you could stop going to camp for a while. You could stay at our house during the day."

"Well, that would be a break—getting out of camp, I mean."

"The doll talked some more last night. We forgot to bring her in, and I went out to get her in the middle of the night. She asked me why I had come and what I wanted to ask. And then she told me she was an oracle, and that she wasn't the doll, but that she was living in the doll. Have you ever heard anything about oracles?"

"Not really. Listen, I've been thinking about this stuff, too. It has got to be a trick of some sort. Some kind of radio or walkie-talkie, something like that. Somebody is wired up to her, somehow."

"But all she has is a voice box. And something else happened, too. You know the old man who lives on our second floor? The white-haired one? He was out on his deck last night, and I saw him when I was bringing the doll inside. He was just standing there staring."

"You probably woke him up."

"I couldn't have. I was so quiet, nobody could hear me."

"You think he's up there spying on you all the time?"

"Well, not spying, but I wonder if he knows something about Gabby. I just found out he's a doll expert. Anita

Russell took some of Megan's dolls to a doll expert at the Children's Museum, and it turned out to be Mr. Edgar."

"I think he sounds weird."

"Listen, why don't you ask your mom to get you out of camp? We can try to find out what the oracle really is. Suppose it tells the future? Think of what we could do, if she really is an oracle. We could know everything that's going to happen. Anywhere! To anybody!"

"I don't know about that. But, okay, I'll ask my mom. But I can't spend the whole summer at your house. My dad is probably going to come to see me, and we'll be spending all our time together."

"Oh. When is that going to happen?"

"I don't know for sure. But soon."

"Why don't you ask the oracle?"

There was a long silence. "So what'd she tell you last night?" James said finally.

"I couldn't think of any good questions right then, but I asked about the weather. She said there would be ice today! And then I asked her if anything exciting was going to happen, and she said somebody would drown."

"Kind of gruesome."

"Yes. That's what she calls 'exciting.' "

"Hmm. Well, listen, Rose. First of all, wait and see if these predictions come true. It's the middle of summer. How can everything freeze over when it's hot? Then, in the meantime, here's what we do. We make my mom think it's *healthy* for us to be playing together. That's not so hard. We'll go in and play Monopoly or something where Cindy can see us, and then she'll tell Mom how well we get along and all that."

"Right. I know what. I'll make some popcorn and we can share it and they'll say we're turning into really good friends."

"You got it."

The plan seemed to be working. They set up the Monopoly board in Cindy's view on the dining-room table, and they kept saying "I really like playing games on a hot afternoon" and "Isn't it great not to have to go outside." Rose wasn't sure Cindy noticed them, though. As soon as they began to play, she picked up a magazine and never once looked over the top of it at their game.

They all jumped when a bolt of lightning sizzled outside the window and a tremendous crack of thunder burst upon their ears.

"Holy smokes! It's about to storm!" Cindy said, throwing down the magazine. "I didn't even notice."

The sky had blackened with the heaviest clouds Rose had ever seen. Huge, swollen masses moved in ominously. She could see darts of lightning playing in the distance, and then another big bolt cracked around their heads. Wind whipped and tore at the yew bushes in the yard, and the leaves on the cherry tree scattered in whirlwinds. The air itself seemed yellowish and purple, as if it were bruised by the pressure of the clouds. Then a strange rattling began on the roof and windows, and there was a constant drumming sound, louder and louder. Small white balls began to fall in the yard, bouncing off the metal chairs on the patio and landing in the grass.

"It's raining mothballs," said Rose, "or rice, or something."

"It's hail," said Cindy. "It's a real, live hailstorm!"

Hail. Hail was ice. "James!" Rose whispered. "Ice. Remember?"

James walked over to the window and looked out, his arms folded across his chest, as if he weren't a bit surprised. "You may have something," he said to Rose, and a smile crept across his face. But Rose was far from smiling. Was the drowning next? Somewhere was someone about to drown? She felt sick.

"Oh my gosh, the windows! Hey, let's get the windows everybody. Quick!" cried Cindy.

The hail was mixing now with big drops of rain, and the wind was rising stronger and stronger. Then the rain fell all at once, so that the world outside was nothing but water rushing down.

"Come on, Rose! James!" Cindy raced around the sun porch, pushing down the heavy windows and yelling. Rose and James dashed from room to room after her, pulling down windows. Cindy grabbed a towel from the bathroom and threw another to Rose, and they began frantically mopping up the window sills and floor. It wasn't until the rain had settled to a steady downpour that anyone thought to wonder where Lucy was. Cindy went from room to room, calling, "Lucy? Lucy?" Soon Rose and James were running with her, shouting, "Lucy! Where are you?"

"I'm down here." They heard a small voice in the distance.

Rose pulled open the basement door. Lucy was sitting calmly on the bottom stair, sucking her thumb and holding a flannel blanket.

"Lucy! Were you scared?" cried Cindy, hurrying down the stairs.

Lucy shook her head. She didn't look the slightest bit scared. "I was down here already, so I stayed down here," she explained.

"What were you doing?" asked Cindy.

"I was helping with the wash."

"You were? What a nice thing to do," said Cindy. Rose ground her teeth. How did Lucy always manage to get noticed when she did something right?

Cindy turned on the light in the laundry room and opened the lid of the washing machine. "Well, my goodness!" she said. "I wouldn't have thought she needed washing so soon."

"What do you mean, *she?*" asked Rose. Suddenly a horrible fear gripped her stomach. She ran over and looked inside the washing machine.

"Lucy! What have you done?" she shrieked. Floating among the towels and their father's underwear was a pink, sodden mass that was Gabby.

"She's not through rinsing yet," Lucy said.

"But she'll be ruined! She's—she's the one! She's drowned!" cried Rose.

"Rose, sweetie, maybe she's washable. Let's see what it says on the tag," Cindy said, fishing out the doll. Gabby's soaked body had lost all its shape. The outlines of her voice box were visible through the wet cloth of her chest. Her hair clung together like a bunch of strings.

"She's only a doll," Cindy said. "And the tag says she's washable. My goodness, you aren't going to cry, are you?" Cindy looked in disbelief at Rose's eyes, filling with tears, and she laughed, not very kindly.

"But I was having fun with her, too," Rose said, trying to give a plausible explanation. She caught sight of Lucy, staring at her in fearful surprise, and of James, who was shaking his head. He said something to himself, but she couldn't hear what.

"Well, look," said Cindy. "The doll will certainly dry out. You can put her right in the dryer. It's only the voice box, the tag says, that's not immersible. That means, don't get it wet. Let's take it out right now and leave it to dry. We'll let the washing machine finish and put the doll in the dryer. Then she'll be good as new."

Cindy wrung out Gabby's arms and legs, unzipped her, took out the voice box, zipped her up again, and dropped her back into the washing machine. She closed the top, and the humming and swishing noise started up. She tilted the voice box one way and then the other, just to test it, but no sound came out. She shrugged and laid it all by itself on top of the dryer between the boxes of laundry soap and the Borax.

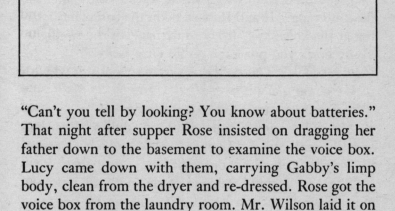

CHAPTER 9

"Can't you tell by looking? You know about batteries." That night after supper Rose insisted on dragging her father down to the basement to examine the voice box. Lucy came down with them, carrying Gabby's limp body, clean from the dryer and re-dressed. Rose got the voice box from the laundry room. Mr. Wilson laid it on the workbench in his shop and turned on the spotlight.

"All we can do is open it up and let it dry out," said Mr. Wilson. "I can't predict the outcome. Either it will work, or it won't. But it isn't the end of the world. If it doesn't work, we can always buy a new one."

"We've got to have this one," Rose said.

"Gabby wants her regular one," Lucy added.

"I'm afraid it's the best I can do," said her father. "You know, we do have more important things to think about these days." He pried the back off the box and removed the battery. The purple and yellow wires sprang out.

Rose thought she heard an extra creak, but it could have been something else in the basement. Maybe it was a mouse.

"We'll give it a week to dry out," said Mr. Wilson. "Now I'm going up to wait for your mother to call." He left the children and the voice box and climbed the stairs to the kitchen.

"You're supposed to wait a whole week?" said James the next morning. He and Rose stood in the basement, looking at the voice box. It lay mute beneath the spotlight. "Why don't you put a fan on it? Or a heater?"

Rose shook her head. "I don't want to fool around with it. We could make it worse."

"Leave it to a little kid to mess things up."

"She didn't know, James, really she didn't." Rose had scarcely ever defended Lucy in her life, and it felt strange. "It'll work again. What did your mom say about camp?"

"She said I could get out of the next session. She already wrote them a letter. That means I'll miss two weeks, starting on Monday. But now what's the point, if this oracle, or whatever it is, is wrecked?" His look plainly put the responsibility on her.

"It's not wrecked," said Rose.

"Look at it! Wires coming out, soaked in the washing machine. Come on! How do you think your TV would do if you put it through the wash?"

"It's not the same."

"I'm just being realistic."

"Why don't you try being patient instead? That's what my dad is always telling us, be more patient."

James shrugged his shoulders. "So that's what your

dad is always telling you. It's boring to be patient. It gets you nowhere. You can't wait around your whole life long."

"Forget about it then," said Rose. "You can go back to your stupid old camp. But when she talks again, don't expect me to tell you about it." *And if she doesn't talk again, if it's all ruined before we even get a good start, and there's nothing left but wires coming out . . .* Tears began to sting and swell behind Rose's nose. She pressed on her nose with the palm of one hand to make herself not cry.

"But I don't want to go back to camp," said James finally. That was all he said.

They had hamburgers again for supper. Mr. Wilson found a box of frozen mixed vegetables in the back of the freezer.

"The last time we had those Mom didn't make us eat them," said Rose.

Mr. Wilson said they would be fine.

"Dad, tonight can we try to get the voice box going?" she asked as her father sat down. She began poking through the vegetables on her plate, looking for kernels of corn among the carrot cubes, lima beans, and peas.

"The what?" Mr. Wilson got up to get the salt and pepper and a handful of paper napkins.

"Lucy's doll's voice box. You know."

"Oh yes." Her father sat down and took a large bite of his hamburger and said, "Onion. Forgot the onion," and got to his feet.

"Can't we try?" Rose pressed on.

"I thought I said to give it a week," her father replied, coming back to the table with a dish full of sliced onions.

"Can't we do it now?"

"Rose, please don't pester me about it! You are going to have to be patient about the noise box or whatever it is, and about things in general for a while. I have too many other things to take care of at the moment. I don't see Lucy worrying about the doll, do I?"

"Gabby feels funny without her voice box," said Lucy. "She doesn't sit up right because her middle caves in."

"Let's not get into the details," said her father. "It will all work out."

"If we don't do the voice box after supper, can we go to Bill's for ice cream?" Lucy asked.

"No! You can have cookies for dessert."

Their father was not acting like his usual patient self. Rose and Lucy both stopped talking and concentrated on dividing their vegetables into edible and inedible.

The cookies were the wrong kind. Their mother never bought these: an enormous red waxy bag of hard, sugary circles with lemon frosting.

"I hope these are the kind you like," said their father. Rose's heart sank, not because the cookies were awful, but because her father suddenly seemed wrong and kind of helpless.

"They're good, Dad," Rose said, taking one and dutifully biting into it.

The telephone rang. Mr. Wilson jumped up to answer it. They were all expecting it to be Mrs. Wilson.

"Oh, hi, Gordon. No, I don't mind being called at home."

Someone from work. "Come on, Luce," Rose said, beckoning to her sister as their father disappeared into the dining room with the telephone. She opened the basement door, went down the stairs to her father's shop, and turned on the spotlight. She peered into the voice box from every angle, turning it one way and another. There was nothing that seemed different from any other time she had looked.

"What are you doing?" asked Lucy.

"I'm going to put this thing back together myself," said Rose.

"But you don't know how."

"I can figure it out. I did it before, on the night before your birthday."

The battery lay nearby on a paper towel. "I wonder if we need a new one," Rose said. She picked it up and shook it. It looked fine. The label was still on it, and it didn't seem waterlogged. Rose snapped the terminals onto the battery, pushed the wires back in as neatly as she could, and pressed with the fingers of both hands. The battery popped right into position. Easy. She turned the back of the voice box the right way around and fitted it in place. Another click, and she was done. "Pretty simple, once you get the hang of it," she said to Lucy. She tilted the voice box from side to side. No sound came out, not even a whisper of a sound. Rose shook it hard. There were little clicks inside, but no voice, no whirring, no "Ma-ma," and certainly no *other* voice.

"I'm going to put it back in Gabby," said Lucy. "Even if it doesn't work, it makes her sit up better." Rose handed the voice box to Lucy.

They found their father emptying the dishwasher at top speed.

"I put it back together myself, Dad," said Rose. "It doesn't work, though."

"I'm going to try your mother in a few minutes. Do you children want to talk to her?"

"She doesn't talk anymore," Lucy said, holding up Gabby.

"I am tired of this talking-doll business!" Mr. Wilson exclaimed. "I don't want to hear any more about it now. Rose, why don't you put the silverware away." He handed her a fistful of forks and spoons. "Lucy, you can put this pot in the bottom cabinet."

Lucy dropped Gabby onto a kitchen chair, where she slumped back, wordless, while Rose and Lucy helped with chores. When the kitchen was tidy, their father dialed Grandma Foley's telephone number. No answer. That meant their mother was at the hospital.

Mr. Wilson began running water for Lucy's bath. Left alone in the kitchen, Rose went over to Gabby and gave her a testing shake. Dead as a doornail.

She was not going to give up. James and her father might have their doubts, but Gabby was going to speak again. It was a good thing her mother wasn't there. Her mother would have said the voice box was ruined right from the start, and she'd have thrown it out. There had to be some fix-it shop that Rose could take it to. Maybe one of those places that sold radios and cassettes and VCRs could repair it. Or a toy fix-it place. Or a doll hospital. Supposedly there were such things.

Rose rustled through the yellow pages of the telephone book, looking under "F" for fix-it and "D" for doll. "Doll Hospital for Tiny Friends. Washburn." Washburn was a suburb, impossible to reach unless you had a car. If ever there was a wrong time to ask her father to drive to Washburn, this was it. "Doll Repair Shop" was the next listing, but it was in a town Rose had never even heard of.

Why wasn't there a doll hospital in the city? Or at least a doll doctor? Then the solution came to her, though she shivered when she remembered the way he had looked, standing on his deck in the dark like a ghost, his silver hair gleaming so brightly. The expert. The doll expert living upstairs. She would ask him to fix it.

The next afternoon at three-thirty James appeared as usual. He slung his damp towel and swimming suit onto the kitchen counter and stuffed himself with Cheez-its and apple juice.

"Where's Cindy?" he asked.

"In the basement with Lucy. My mom has a sewing machine down there, and Cindy's helping Lucy make a doll blanket for you-know-who." She nodded toward Gabby, who sat in one of the kitchen chairs, silently staring at the rim of the table.

"Tomorrow's my last day of camp," he said. "Sure hope there'll be something to do around here." He gave Rose a significant look.

"Guess what," said Rose.

"What?"

"We put the box back in."

"And so?"

"It doesn't work. Yet."

"Yet! Rose, you're gonna turn a hundred years old just waiting for that thing to work again."

"No I'm not. You know what I'm going to do?"

"What."

"I'm going to take it up to Mr. Edgar and see if he can fix it."

"You mean that guy who was spying on you?"

"Yes. Mrs. Russell said he was a doll expert. If he works at the Children's Museum, he must be good at fixing dolls."

"He's kind of spooky, don't you think? You're going to just take it to him? How do you know what he'll do with it?"

"I don't care if he's spooky."

"All right." James shrugged his shoulders. He was trying to look as if he didn't care one way or the other, but Rose saw a flush start across his freckled cheeks. He was getting interested again. "So let's go," he said.

"Now?" Rose had imagined herself talking to the spare, white-haired man at some indeterminate time, preferably accompanied by her father. "I wasn't going to do it now."

"Why not now? Isn't he home?"

Rose took a deep breath. "Let's go ring his bell and find out," she said. One thing about James was, he didn't waste time.

They walked around the house to Mr. Edgar's entrance, and Rose pressed the bell. She heard it ring inside the hallway. She waited and pressed the bell again. No footsteps. Nobody home.

"Not here," said Rose cheerfully. "Probably at work. Well, I'll go up to see him tonight with my dad."

"Let's take Gabby to the museum."

"Well, I mean—do what?"

"Take the doll to the old guy at the museum right now."

"By ourselves?"

"Sure. I can take the T. I've done it for years."

From the way he said "T," instead of "MBTA" or "subway," Rose knew James must be an old hand at riding public transportation.

"Isn't it a long way?"

"I've never actually gone to the museum, but so what if it is? You aren't scared to go, are you?"

"I'm not the one who's scared."

"Okay. Then let's go. We'll leave a note for Cindy."

"Shouldn't we ask her first?"

"Suppose she says no. You know she's not going to say yes. This way we don't have to do something we were just told not to do."

"How much does it cost?"

"A quarter."

"My dad'll kill me when he finds out," said Rose.

Rose stuffed Gabby into Lucy's bag, which she found hanging on a hook near the back door, and James wrote the note:

Dear Cindy.
Rose and I are going to the Children's Museum.
DONT WORRY. Home by dinner—J.
P.S. DONT WORRY. I can take the T by myself.

James anchored the note with the sugar bowl, and he and Rose went out the door and turned onto the street.

Rose could feel the doll bumping against her leg. They were walking fast, in case Cindy happened to look for them before they got to the corner. Rose wondered if someone would mug them right away. She tightened her grip on the bag and looked over her shoulder and across the street. Nobody.

James said they could wait for the streetcar on the other side of Center Street in front of the pizza place. Rose could see a bunch of teenagers up ahead, standing around Earl's Pharmacy on the corner. She and James were going to have to pass the teenagers in order to cross the street. A grocery-store dumpster occupied two-thirds of the little lot beside Earl's. It smelled of garbage. Strewn around and stuck in the straggly bushes and weeds beside the paving were pieces of melon rind, Styrofoam trays sticky with meat juice, paper wrappers from candy, and rotten bits of vegetables. Rose recognized a green pepper.

"Yuck, this place always stinks," she said.

The bunch of teenagers closed up as Rose and James approached. They were smoking cigarettes and snapping gum.

"Goin' to the store for Mama?" said one of them.

"What a good little boy and girl!" said another, laughing.

"Look at Jack and Jill, goin' up the hill."

"Aw, let 'em go through," said a boy, blowing a stream of cigarette smoke over Rose's head. James ignored them and pushed the Walk-light button. The Walk light stayed on long enough for them to get just halfway across Center Street. Then it flicked off, and the waiting line of cars surged forward. James grabbed Rose by the shoulder and hurried her to the curb. They waited for ten minutes by the yellow trolley sign in front of the pizza shop before they saw the streetcar swaying toward them. Rose was sure Anita Russell would drive by while they were standing there and insist that they go right home. But no one noticed them at all.

James climbed on first and dropped their quarters in the meter. They swung down the aisle, clutching at the backs of seats as the car started up, and fell onto a bench.

"That was the worst part," said James. "Now nobody can stop us till we get there. See? It was easy."

"Right." Rose squeezed the top edges of Lucy's bag together. The last familiar storefront slid out of view.

"Where do we get off?" she asked James.

"We stay on this till we get to Park, then we change to the Red Line. See, on the map there? Then it's two stops, and we're there."

"How do you know when we get to Park?"

"It'll say so, right on the walls."

"What walls?" asked Rose, looking out at the tops of cars beside them in traffic.

"The subway walls. What else? You know the streetcar goes on top of the street till we get to Northeastern, and then it goes underground on the subway tracks. Haven't you ever been on the Green Line?"

"I have, but only a couple of times with my dad, and I didn't pay attention."

"You haven't been anywhere by yourself, have you."

"You don't have to sound so disgusted, James."

"Well, you haven't, have you."

"Not to Park Street."

"Just do what I tell you to."

More and more people got on, crowding up against Rose's knees. Purses and shopping bags rustled and pressed close to her face. The trolley hurtled into an underground tunnel. It stopped at a couple of stations and even more crowds pushed into the car. The window in back of Rose's head was partway open, and a hot, metallic smell came in with the rush of wind. It occurred to Rose, as they were jostling and bumping along, that she didn't know for sure that Mr. Edgar was at the museum.

"Are you sure you'll be able to tell when it's our stop?" Rose asked.

"Don't worry. When everybody gets off, we get off, too," James said.

Yellow lights flashed by periodically as the car rocked along its dark path.

"This is almost it," James said, twisting around to look in back of him.

"Boylston—Boylston—Boylston," read the signs on the walls. The trolley stopped, started again, and surged ahead to the next stop. James was on his feet and moving toward the door while they were slowing down. "Now. Here we are," he said. The car stopped with another screech. James vanished.

Rose stood up in a forest of human bodies, all of them taller than she was, all of them pushing toward the doors. For a moment she thought she couldn't breathe. Then, beneath a man's elbow, she glimpsed the window, and outside it stood James, waiting for her. She began to shove forward, grinding her teeth, stepping on someone's foot, squeezing between two men wearing running suits. Then, like toast from a toaster, she popped out of the trolley and onto the platform.

"Now we've got to find the Red Line," said James.

The station was swarming with people, and garbled announcements were being made over the PA system. Lurid lights shone from little newspaper shops, and in every direction were exits and entrances, turnstiles and filthy green tile corridors, and signs marked "Inbound" and "Outbound." Clusters of people stood beside the tracks or sat on benches, shepherding shopping bags and briefcases with their knees.

"Guess it's rush hour," said James. "Start looking for the Red Line Outbound." Rose stood still and looked dizzily around.

"Go ask over there," said James.

Rose saw what looked like a policeman sitting in a square booth. There was a window on each side of the booth and a dim sign—Information—on each window. They walked all around the booth and picked a window. Rose stepped up. "How do we get to the Children's Museum?" she asked.

"YoutaketheRedLineanycaratalltoSouthStationhaveaniceday," said the man, pointing over Rose's head. She couldn't understand him, but she turned to where he pointed, and there it was: Red Line Outbound.

They began to run, not knowing why, except that hurrying made it seem more likely that they would get there. Rose thought James was looking kind of worried. "Is something the matter?" she asked.

"Not really. It's just that I forgot. We'll have to pay

to get into the museum. I didn't bring any money."

There were more people coming out of the museum than going into it when Rose and James got to the tall glass entrance doors. The Children's Museum was one of Rose and Lucy's favorite places. It was full of things children could put their hands on or walk into or use: life-size models of old-fashioned houses, of city streets above and below ground, of dentist's and doctor's offices. There was a real Japanese house and a real television studio. It usually was a friendly, bustling place. Now it seemed faintly foreboding.

"It isn't closed, is it?" Rose asked.

"We better get in there and find out," said James. "We still have to make them let us in, you know."

"What if Mr. Edgar isn't here? We don't know if he's here."

"Don't worry about that now, Rose. Here's what we do. Say we have this appointment, and we aren't going to look at anything in the museum, we're just going straight up to see Mr. Edgar, but we forgot our card. Pretend I'm your brother, or your uncle, or something."

"You want *me* to say all that?"

"You say it, because he's your neighbor, not mine."

"But they'll be able to tell I'm lying!"

"They won't. Rose, you're chickening out. I should have known you'd do that."

Rose flounced away from James, marched through the entrance, and headed for a long counter near the door. A lady in a red jacket was standing guard there, smiling pleasantly.

"My brother and I have this appointment, and we

aren't going to look at anything in the museum. So can we go in? We don't have our membership card."

"I beg your pardon?"

"We have an appointment. We're going to see Mr. Edgar about my doll, but we forgot our card. Can we get in anyhow?" Making up stories wasn't so hard, once you got into it. Rose tried to make herself sound a little younger and a little more helpless than she really was.

The lady's smile grew even larger, and she crinkled her eyes. "With whom is your appointment?" she asked.

"Mr. Edgar. I have a doll for him to look at." Rose opened the top of the bag for the lady to see.

The lady looked in and seemed relieved. "I'm sure Mr. Edgar is just the person to see. I'll tell him you're here."

"Oh, never mind, don't do that. We'll just go on in."

"He doesn't like to have people walk in without being announced. You did arrange to see him, didn't you?"

"He knows me, because he lives in my house," Rose said. "We've just been so worried about my doll, and he can fix it, I'm sure."

"Well, all right then." The lady looked tired. "It's only fifteen minutes till closing time, so you'd better hurry. Third floor—"

Rose didn't hear the rest of what she said, because she and James were already running up the broad central staircase to the second floor, and they kept climbing. Over the stair railing Rose could see the half-deserted exhibits: the Indian Tepee, Your Dentist's Office, Grandmotner's Attic. A huge telephone and giant's desk top sprawled below on her left: A toddler in shorts was just climbing out of the paper-clip box on the desk. Up on the third floor, they walked down the hall past the glass case with Monopoly games in every language and past the room with twenty dollhouses.

Staff Only—blue letters were spaced across the door they wanted. James opened it. Ahead of them stretched a corridor. The plate-glass windows on both sides looked into storage rooms, a library, and—at the end—the doll workshop. The door was partway open. Rose and James pushed it back with a creak and found themselves face-to-face with a mild-looking, white-haired man. He was wearing a threadbare sweater and sitting behind a cluttered desk.

"I've been expecting you," said Mr. Edgar.

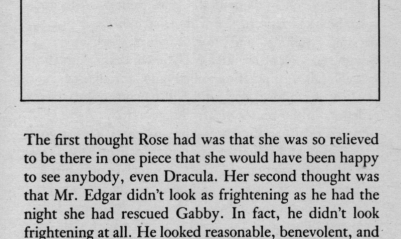

CHAPTER 10

The first thought Rose had was that she was so relieved to be there in one piece that she would have been happy to see anybody, even Dracula. Her second thought was that Mr. Edgar didn't look as frightening as he had the night she had rescued Gabby. In fact, he didn't look frightening at all. He looked reasonable, benevolent, and old. His face was not wrinkled, though, so it was hard to say what made him look old. Maybe it was his silver hair, maybe his threadbare sweater.

"This is my friend, James," said Rose.

James nodded, but did not smile.

"You knew we were coming?" asked Rose.

"I thought you probably would come. But tell me what you've come for."

"My sister has this doll," Rose said, reaching into the bag for Gabriella. As she was talking, she kept looking around, trying to take in everything she saw. The little office was crammed with stacks of papers and magazines, tiny bottles of glue and paint; scraps of wood, foam rubber, cloth, and leather; sequins and beads in tiny dishes; and miniature yellow, green, and purple feathers. The door behind Mr. Edgar's cluttered desk opened into a big workroom where huge tables were spread with whole dolls and parts of dolls.

"This doll is a talking doll," Rose went on. "It's got a voice box and batteries. But my sister threw it into the washing machine, and now it won't work anymore. Could you look at it and see if you think it's ruined, or if it will talk again?" Rose pulled out Gabriella, who still smelled of laundry soap, and laid her on top of a stack of letters in the center of Mr. Edgar's desk.

"Let's take her into my shop, where I have a good light," said Mr. Edgar, putting on a pair of half-glasses and adjusting them on his nose. He picked up Gabriella as carefully as if she were alive and took her through the door to a long, high table in his shop. Rose and James followed. The other tables were stacked with doll wigs and doll arms and doll dresses, as well as with stuffed animals in various stages of shabbiness and fadedness. Some of the animals were missing their head or an ear or had a tear in their fur, which let the stuffing spill out. Clamps held some dolls captive. The arm of a sewing machine swam above a sea of fabric.

"Have you ever seen a doll like this before?" asked Rose.

"Every doll is different, even if it's manufactured by the thousand," said Mr. Edgar. He placed the doll under a low-hanging worklight and turned on the switch. Gabriella was flooded with light. Rose noticed that Mr.

Edgar's hands were trembling slightly, and he seemed to be short of breath, as if he were suddenly anxious about the doll. He unzipped Gabby, took out the voice box and removed its cover. Then he undid a tiny screw with a miniature screw driver and took out the metal mechanism that produced Gabby's voice.

"There's no rust here," he said. "It works by the music box principle, only it uses weights. You tip the box, and it winds itself so that it can talk for a short run. I see nothing to indicate that it won't work again once the residual dampness has evaporated. But I have some special oil I'll put in. And I'll clean the battery terminals." He began oiling and rubbing the voice box with tiny cloths. "What does this doll say?" he asked casually.

"She says . . . she says . . ." Rose's tongue stuck, for while Mr. Edgar's question had sounded casual, a look had come into his face that stunned her into silence. He was suddenly staring and watchful, as he had been that night, and she felt the same thrill of fright that she had felt then.

"She says 'Ma-ma' and 'Hi-ya,' " James said. "Just the usual doll talk."

Mr. Edgar did not say anything back. Neither of the children spoke, either, and the long silence became practically unbearable. Mr. Edgar was nearly as peculiar as their mother had said he was, Rose thought.

But of course he was staring at her because he knew what she hadn't said. Did he know she had seen him that night? Of course he did. They were all three pretending that things were different from the way they actually were.

"She says more than 'Ma-ma'," Rose began at last.

"The thing about this doll is . . . we came all this way because . . . she has special powers. She says things that aren't on her voice box, and then the things come true. She makes predictions."

Mr. Edgar's hands stopped trembling. Kindliness shone out of his face like a beam of light. It was as if he had just switched it on. He sat down on a high stool and nodded calmly. "I know a little something about this subject," he said. "Won't you tell me more?"

"Well, it all started when my little sister Lucy got the doll for her birthday, and the very first night she had it, it spoke to her upstairs. And then a couple of days later it said a few more things, and the day after that we had it out under the cherry tree in the backyard, and it said that our mom was leaving, and it said DRIPPING BLOOD. Later that day this friend of mine fell and cut open his forehead right when I was looking. And there was all the dripping blood. Then my grandma got very sick, and right afterward my mother left. So then James started coming to our house because his baby-sitter was watching my sister and me. Then this really strange thing happened. We took the doll out to this green bush in the backyard. You know which one? It's the one way in back by the garage. I used to have a secret hideout there. When we got in it, a hideous snake—I mean it was really big and ugly—came at us and tried to chase us away. We ran out of there and James killed it."

"I wasn't going to at first," James said. "I grabbed a shovel and the next thing I knew I had cut off its head. It died so fast, you couldn't believe it was real. And then after that we went back into the place under the bush, and the doll really started talking. She said she was ours, now that the snake was dead. And she said that the spirit of prophecy was back again, or something like that."

"She said that?" asked Mr. Edgar eagerly. "That proves it then. What you have told me, about the snake in particular, absolutely convinces me. What you have here is not a talking doll. It's an oracle. And not just any oracle, either. I believe, in fact, that it is the Oracle of Delphi, which has now re-emerged through this doll. Classical oracles, you know, had many ways of speaking—through priestesses, rustling oak leaves, rattling stones, children, or birds. There's no reason why an oracle couldn't use a doll, especially one that already had a voice. So she's found! Found again! Do you know, by the way, about the people who used to live in your house many, many years before your family moved there?"

"They were some kind of nuns, or sisters who acted like nuns, I think."

"It was a small religious group—some people called it a cult—that lived there. The members practiced an Eastern religion that involved rites and rituals. They cultivated foreign plants—your yard is full of them—and they tried to divine the future. Naturally, they weren't very popular in the neighborhood. After a few years they went back to their native country. But some of the plants they put in, such as the green bush you were telling me about, still grow behind your house."

"Why weren't they popular?" asked Rose, though when she tried to imagine her mother liking them, she had a pretty good idea.

"They kept to themselves, and they seemed odd to

other people. They spoke a foreign language, and I suppose they were not very friendly with anyone outside their group. Anyway, I believe that a combination of the special plant in your yard plus the constant seeking for the spirit of divination has finally paid off—only the people who wanted the oracle most have long since gone. And you are the one who has discovered it, and therefore you now possess it."

"Me and my sister and James," said Rose, who suddenly did not want to be stuck with the oracle by herself.

"All three of you," said Mr. Edgar. "There is a myth that the Oracle of Delphi was originally guarded by a terrible serpent, the Python. One of the earliest feats of the god Apollo was to kill the Python. Then the oracle belonged to him. He was the god of music and divination. I've never heard of an oracle belonging to a plain human being, much less a child. Or even three children. It's quite a responsibility, you know."

"My dad told me a little bit about oracles," said Rose. "But he said they were only around a long time ago, in ancient days."

"The classical era of ancient Greece and Rome was a period when prophecy was especially strong," said Mr. Edgar. "But these forms of energy survive, even though their power is greatly reduced."

"Even if it's reduced, can we ask it anything, and will it tell us?" asked James.

"Yes. It knows everything," said Mr. Edgar. "And what it says always comes to pass, even though it doesn't always happen exactly as the listener expects it to. A person might spend his entire life trying to avoid the fate that the oracle predicted for him, but, in the end, the prediction will always come true."

James and Rose looked at each other and then at the doll, just lying there on the table, staring up.

"May I ask what you are planning to do with her?" Mr. Edgar said.

"Well, we were just going to keep her around and ask her the future and things like that," said James.

Mr. Edgar picked up the doll and zipped the voice box into her back and straightened her dress and sat her against a stack of books.

"You plan to keep her for a few days or weeks, perhaps?"

"For longer than that!" Rose exclaimed. "For good! At least until we grow up."

"I was only asking, because you may find her burdensome. I would be glad to take her off your hands if that should be the case."

"How could she be burdensome?" asked Rose indignantly. "She's only a little doll. We can ask her questions in the daytime and take her in at night." She shrugged her shoulders.

"If more snakes turn up, I can take care of them," James added.

"Aha!" said Mr. Edgar. "Let's think a moment. It is important to use an oracle well, and it is equally important to guard her. You must keep her a secret. If others know about her powers, they will surely want her for themselves. Imagine the consequences if the oracle should get into the wrong hands. Think of the danger."

"I'm trying, but I can't think of any," said Rose.

"Suppose someone got the oracle away from you and set himself up as a predictor of the future. Think of the power that person could wield once other people knew about him. He could sell his predictions. He could withhold predictions until people did what he wanted. Other people would certainly try to steal the oracle from him. They could become very nasty to one another. They could even murder one another. Or start a war over it."

"But how could someone else get control of the oracle, if it belongs to us?" asked Rose.

"What if he kidnapped you?"

"How come you know so much about this stuff?" asked James.

"I just happen to be interested in the subject," said Mr. Edgar. "It's like a hobby for me."

"We can keep it a secret," Rose said. "I never tell anything when I've promised not to."

"It may not be that simple," said Mr. Edgar. "Suppose you ask the oracle about—say, an earthquake, and the oracle tells you there's going to be one in a particular place. What will you do?"

"Tell the people who live there, of course."

"How?"

"I don't know. Tell the newspapers, call the TV stations."

"Crackpots do that all the time."

Rose was silent.

"Suppose we used it just for ourselves," said James.

"Then the question to consider is whether you really want to know the future. You will not always get an answer that pleases you. And knowing the future will not change it."

"If we want to know the future, we want to know it, that's all, and we can figure out what to do about it. I mean, if we found the oracle, shouldn't we use it? Isn't that what it's for?" said Rose.

"Finders keepers," added James.

"No one ever entirely possesses an oracle," said Mr. Edgar.

"Even if we only sort of possess it, then." Rose was beginning to get annoyed. "What do *you* think we should do with it?"

"If I were you—" Mr. Edgar stopped.

"If you were us, what?"

"Well." Mr. Edgar leaned toward them. "Have you considered destroying it?"

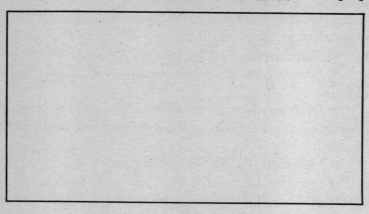

CHAPTER 11

"No, and you can't make us," Rose said in a shaky voice.

"Of course not! Heavens! But that is one possibility. Destroy it, or else give it to someone who can devote himself entirely to it and nothing else."

Rose had the distinct sense that she had suddenly stepped in over her head. Mr. Edgar looked menacing again. The kindly glow had vanished from his face and been replaced with a look of watchful, hostile concentration. The thought crossed her mind that there were other things that Mr. Edgar wasn't telling them.

"We're going to pack her up now," said Rose.

"You will find that she talks again," said Mr. Edgar.

"We have to go home now," said Rose. She wanted to get out of there as fast as she could. What if Mr. Edgar convinced her to do something she didn't want to do? Like give him the doll to dispose of? *He wants this doll for himself*, she thought. *Maybe he's the one who wants to sell her predictions and become powerful.* Rose picked up Gabby and dropped her into Lucy's bag.

"I suppose it's your suppertime," Mr. Edgar said. The way he pronounced "suppertime" made it sound as if he had never heard of eating supper.

"My dad'll be wondering where I am," said Rose, inching sideways toward the door.

"Remember this," Mr. Edgar said to her, trying to sound friendly again. "I am always available to help you with your doll, if you have any more questions about her. Guard her well! I know about a great many things, and you are the kind of children who can learn . . . ."

By now Rose had gotten herself out the door, and she turned and raced down the corridor, with James panting close behind her. They pushed through the Staff Only door at the same moment and hurried on. Only after the door had swung shut did they realize they were in the dark. The lights in the exhibit rooms had been turned off. A dim safety light shone in the broad hallway.

"The museum's closed," said James.

"Uh-oh."

"We have to find the way back to the front door."

"Maybe we can see better up ahead."

They walked slowly down the dark, silent corridor. Midway, a small overhead light shone down upon the central staircase. They made their way down the steps.

"Hello there?" called a voice from below. Rose and James jumped. Light was coming into the staircase from the first floor entrance, and they could see a uniformed guard standing by the bottom steps.

"Can we get out?" James called back. "We were up-

• *109*

stairs having a meeting with Mr. Edgar."

"With who?" asked the guard. Now that they were close up, Rose could see the shiny gold stripe on the brim of his hat. It said "Security." On his pocket was an embroidered strip that said "Walter J. Bryant."

"Mr. Edgar. About this doll here," said James.

"What've you got in your bag there?" asked the guard.

"That's it, the doll." Rose opened Lucy's canvas bag once again. "She used to be a talking doll until my sister threw her into the washing machine, and then she wouldn't talk anymore. So we took her to Mr. Edgar to fix."

"Uh-huh. And did he?"

"Yes. He oiled her and he says she'll talk again."

"That's all right then," said the guard. "I'll unlock the door for you. You have a way home now?"

"We can take the subway," said James.

Rose was about to ask for a ride, a taxi, anything to get her out of there.

"You sure?" asked the guard.

"That's how we got here," said James.

"All right then. Take care." The guard flipped through his ring of keys until he came to the one he wanted. He fitted it into the door, turned the handle, and had just worked it open when a blurred, quivering voice called, HELP! HELP ME!

"What's that?" The guard was instantly alert.

"James! She's working!" cried Rose. "It's just my doll," she said to the guard.

"A doll that says 'help'? That's a strange thing for a doll to say."

HELP! came the voice again, this time with a watery, bubbling noise for punctuation.

"Doesn't she say 'Ma-ma'?" asked the guard. "How come she doesn't say 'Ma-ma'? Let me see that thing." He took Gabby out and held her at arm's length, squeezing her in the middle. She made a choking sound and then gasped, "Ma-ma!"

"Sounds like a sheep," the guard said.

Rose bristled. "Would you please give her back?" she snapped.

Gabby hiccupped.

The guard relocked the door. "You know what? I don't know if you kids are up to some kind of trick, but I'm not letting you out of the museum till I know what's going on here. Now why don't you give me your parents' phone numbers, and we'll call them up, and we can have a little meeting together about this. This is just too strange for Walter J. Bryant. And I'm going to buzz Mr. Edgar, and he'll tell me if all this is on the up and up. I don't mean to scare you, but here we have this doll and it's shouting for help!"

Gabby's voice box was coughing and choking. "Do you suppose she needs artificial respiration?" Rose whispered to James.

"Give her a thump on the back," James answered.

There was nothing they could do about the guard. He buzzed Mr. Edgar, but there was no answer. Naturally, that made him all the more suspicious. They gave him the Wilsons' phone number, and in less time than she could have supposed or wished Rose saw the familiar dusty brown Toyota pull up in the circular museum driveway. Out came her father, looking mad as hops.

"Whatever happens," Rose muttered to James, "I am not giving up Gabby."

Rose's father was perfectly polite while they were in the museum. He assured the guard that the children were innocent of any tricks, and, yes, it was just a talking doll, though an eccentric one, to be sure. He bundled Rose and James into the car. "We're going to discuss this when we get home," he said. "At length."

Mr. Wilson dropped James off in front of his house. "Your mother is waiting for you," he said sternly to the boy. "She's been just as worried as I have." Rose could see Linda standing in the doorway, her hands on her hips. She looked cross, and she began scolding James before he had even climbed the front stairs.

Lucy grabbed the tote bag from Rose as soon as Rose stepped into the front hall. "I want my doll back! Is she in my bag?"

"Be careful! She's working again," Rose called as Lucy ran away with her.

Mr. Wilson told Cindy she could go home now, and he thanked her for the extra hours. "No problem," she said. "Glad the travelers are home again. You two are in deep trouble!" she said to Rose, but Rose thought she saw a twinkle in her eye. Then the lecture began. "What is the story?" Mr. Wilson said. "How many times have your mother and I warned you? The city is not a place for children simply to wander around in. I'm surprised at both of you. I thought you had common sense. Imagine what a scare you've given me, and James's mother, and Cindy."

Rose felt responsibility and guilt drench her from head to toe. She wilted. "I was afraid you'd be mad and worried," Rose said. "But we had to go. We just had to. We had to find out if Mr. Edgar could fix Gabby."

"Mr. Edgar? Our tenant? The one who lives upstairs?"

"Yes. That's him. He fixes dolls at the Children's Museum."

"Why didn't you just take it upstairs then? You didn't need to go all the way downtown."

"We tried," said Rose, "but he wasn't home."

"You could have waited till later."

"We didn't know when he would be there. And James knows about riding the subways. He knew we wouldn't get lost. And we know not to talk to strangers. Gad, we've known that ever since we were two years old."

"If your mother were here—" Mr. Wilson's voice already sounded a little less stern, a little more sorrowful.

"She'd have twenty cat fits," said Rose.

"She would, and rightly so," her father said. "I'm not going to mention this to her, though. She has enough to worry about as it is."

"Grandma isn't worse, is she?"

"I'm afraid she is."

"Did Mom call?"

"While you were gone."

"What did she say?"

"The doctors are not hopeful that Grandma Foley will recover. They don't know what the outcome will be."

"Does that mean she'll die?" Rose could hardly make herself say the word.

"She's very old, Rose."

"How old? Only eighty, isn't she?"

"Eighty is usually thought of as old."

"But she's plain eighty, not eighty-five."

"We'll just have to see, won't we."

Rose felt a second wave of sickening responsibility, even though she knew this had nothing to do with her. If she had stayed home all afternoon, that would not have made Grandma Foley better. And Gabriella would not have gotten oiled and treated, and she would probably not be talking now. Rose *had* made the right decision, she knew she had, even though her father told her she was irresponsible and thoughtless. But knowing this didn't make Rose feel better.

Mr. Wilson's lecture went on and on, and after a while Rose realized that he wasn't angry anymore. He ended by declaring that she was not to go anywhere for two weeks: grounded. No trips to Bill's, no movies, no bike rides. James's camp was already cancelled, so he had to come every day, but Mr. Wilson was going to check with James's mother and see if she agreed to the same punishment. No swimming, no nothing.

"—up to bed early," her father concluded. "And tomorrow I want you to apologize to Cindy for causing her so much worry."

Rose nodded. She tried to keep looking solemn, as if she were digesting the justice of this. In fact, she was mentally jumping for joy. Two weeks straight with the oracle. What more did they need? They would guard the doll well, all right. And treat it properly, too. As for destroying it, or giving it up—why should they? They wouldn't get rid of it. They would keep it forever.

Overhead, footsteps crossed the hallway on the second floor. Mr. Edgar was home now, too.

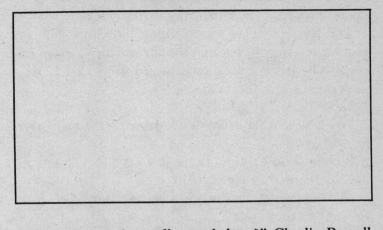

CHAPTER 12

"You mean you're really stuck here?" Charlie Russell asked. It was Monday, and he and Megan had come up to the Wilsons' house on a pair of new bicycles. They were ten-speed bikes with wheels as thin as wires. Charlie's bike was maroon, and Megan's was silver. They looked terrifically speedy. Rose, James, and Lucy were sitting on the grass in the backyard, trying to look completely bored.

"For two weeks, starting last Friday. We can't go anywhere," said Rose.

"We've got new bikes. Ten-speeds. So we came over to see if you want to go riding." Megan's green-and-white-striped shirt reflected green bars onto the bottom of her chin.

"We can't go anywhere, and we're not supposed to have anybody play here, either," said Rose.

"What'd you do?" asked Megan eagerly.

"We went to the Children's Museum by ourselves,

without asking. So everybody got all worked up about it, and now we have to stay home. James has to, too, because we have the same baby-sitter right now."

The Russells' bikes were shining and clean, and the gears made smooth clicking sounds as Charlie spun his pedal. Charlie's cut was nearly healed. It had left a shiny pink ridge on his forehead.

"Nice bikes," said Lucy.

"We got them Saturday," said Megan. "Don't you have anything new?"

It crossed Rose's mind to say just what they did have, but she thought better of it.

"Are you going away now?" Lucy piped up. "We have to work on the shrine."

"Lucy, let's not talk about it," said Rose.

"The shrine?" asked Charlie.

"It's a game we invented so we'd have something to do," said Rose.

"It's not a game. It's for real," said Lucy.

"Can I see it?" asked Megan. "What is it?"

"No!" said Lucy. "Nobody can see it. It's only for us."

"It's real to her," Rose said. "She can't tell the difference between real and pretending yet."

"It's real to you, too!" Lucy protested.

Rose shrugged, as if to say there was no accounting for little kids.

"Well, guess we better go," said Charlie, sitting astride his bike, balancing on one foot. "Have fun with your shrine or whatever."

"I want to see it," repeated Megan. "Hey, what are those flowers for?"

"Oh, come on, Meg, let's go," said Charlie.

"I'm going to come by later and see it," Megan said. She wobbled across the yard after her brother.

"Well, that was a close one," said Rose, when the Russells were out of sight. "Lucy, how many times do I have to tell you: Don't talk about it!"

"I'm not. Only a little bit."

"The Russells are exactly the wrong people to tell, even a little bit."

Lucy didn't reply. Then a smile spread across her face. "Isn't it time?" she asked.

"Okay by me," said James.

"Let's wait just a minute and make sure they don't come back," said Rose.

This morning they were finally ready to try their first ceremony of questions. They had been secretly working on the oracle's cave ever since last Friday, when the punishment began. Rose had told Lucy and James that if they were going to be Gabby's guardians, they ought to treat her properly, the way an oracle should be treated. The problem was, they didn't know how. They spent Friday clearing out all the extra twigs and dried leaves from beneath the special bush so that the space would be clean and smooth. Rose found a small piece of worn-out yellow carpet in the storage room in the basement, and they spread that on the ground at the far end of the cave. Then what?

On Saturday morning Rose told her father that she and James and Lucy were going to spend their two weeks doing a study project on oracles, just as though they were in school. "We aren't going to sit around and waste our time," she said. "So can we borrow some of your books? The ones you said you still had?"

"I always did think I'd find a use for these someday," Mr. Wilson said, looking pleased. He produced a stack of his old college paperback books that he had saved for over twenty years. "My entire collection from Mythology 300. These will certainly keep you busy."

The children took the stack of books out to the yard and began turning through them. "I can't read these," said Lucy.

"That's no surprise," said Rose. The books weren't that easy even for older children like herself, and they didn't have illustrations, either. A picture of the oracle would have been a big help. "Now, let's see. Delphi, Oracle of," said James, running his finger down the index at the back of one fat volume. "Oh, brother. There's dozens of pages here." He began flipping through. "Looks like everybody went to the sacred shrine of Apollo. That's what they call it here."

"Does it say anything about how the shrine looked?" asked Rose. "Was the priestess in special clothes? What did people say to her when they asked her to tell them the future?"

"It doesn't say," said James, scanning several more pages. "There's a million stories here, but it doesn't say anything about clothes or what she looked like. She always sat on a tripod, though. It has to be a tripod."

"What is that?" asked Rose.

"Something with three legs," said James.

"We already have one of those," said Rose. "And we can make up the rest."

"Mr. Edgar probably knows what the shrine looked like," said Lucy.

"We aren't going to ask him anything," said Rose.

They put the three-legged stool in the center of one end of the carpet and placed the plastic dish of pebbles nearby. They decided that the person asking the question should sit at the far end of the carpet, and he or she would put an offering to Gabriella in front of the oracle's tripod. One of Mr. Wilson's books mentioned the heaps of offerings left by pilgrims at the sacred shrine.

"Where will we get all these offerings?" said James.

Rose shook her head. "We'll have to do the best we can with only three of us. Why don't we each give her something whenever it's our turn to ask a question?"

"What'll we give her?" asked Lucy. "Something to eat? Like raisins?"

"What would she do with raisins?" hooted James.

"Well, I like them," Lucy said.

"If we leave food out here, raccoons will probably get it," said Rose. "The oracle isn't like Santa Claus's reindeer, Lucy."

"How about flowers?" asked Lucy.

"That's perfect," said Rose.

"You're on," James agreed.

They had spent the rest of Saturday settling the details, and Rose and Lucy had restlessly endured a Sunday of family chores. Then on Monday the three had been about to begin when the Russells had ridden up the driveway. Lucy had picked some blue bachelor's buttons and some dandelions and tied them together with a piece of string. They looked nice, Rose thought, even if they were weeds.

Rose had broken off a few branches from the bush and woven them into a miniature wreath. The Russells hadn't noticed it lying on the grass.

"It's safe now," said James. "Let's go." Lucy ran into the house and came back out with Gabby. Rose put the wreath on Gabby's head. One at a time they crawled into the cave, and Lucy balanced the doll on her tripod. They arranged themselves in front of her.

"Who's going to be first?" asked James.

"I am," said Lucy.

That seemed fair. Lucy sat on her knees, squarely in front of the doll, and said, "Hello, Oracle. Here is a present." She set the bunch of flowers before Gabby. "Is it okay to ask now?" she said, looking anxiously back at Rose and James.

"Go, Lucy,"said James.

"Okay. When is my mother coming home?"

Rose never forgot those next five minutes. The fragrance within the leafy cave intensified. They were sitting all crouched every which way, and Rose's legs were soon aching and cramped; she heard little twigs crackle and felt sweat trickle down her neck and arms. Everything was green and still and pulsing with summer heat. And then the doll spoke, in a voice so self-assured that Rose's body froze and then prickled all over. It was a new voice, melodious and clear, though the features of her face had not changed: the same half-pleasant smile drawing her hard cheeks into dimples; the same painted blue eyes, with their eyelashes printed above and below; the same infant gaze, forever cheerfully expectant; the same little puckered rosy-red mouth. The oracle said: A PAIR WILL GO, AND THEN SHE'LL COME.

Lucy turned and whispered to Rose and James. "Is that her answer? What does she mean?"

A breeze blew through the green cave, and Gabby looked like an ordinary doll again, an almost-ordinary doll wearing a wreath.

"A pear? An apple?" said James.

"A pair? Like two of something?" said Rose.

The answer was mystifying, but the oracle spirit had clearly retreated, and it didn't seem like a good idea to try to shake it out again.

"Maybe we'll figure it out as we go along," said James.

Rose was thinking something else: What if the answer had been "tomorrow" or "next week"?

James took his turn next. He had made Gabby a bracelet out of aluminum foil to which he had glued colored bits of plastic all around the edge. "James, it's so pretty!" Lucy said.

James set the bracelet before Gabby. "O Gabriella," he said, "the doll who knows everything, what will the score of the Red Sox game be this afternoon?" Again, it seemed that the spicy, evergreen smell grew stronger, as if fumes were pouring out, and gradually the doll's unmoving face became full of attention.

THE PEBBLES SPEAK, was her answer.

Before they had time to wonder what this meant, the plastic dish full of stones rattled around, as though a hand had shaken it. None of them had touched it. When the bowl was still, they sat without moving, waiting to see if anything else was going to happen. The evergreen fragrance began to fade. James leaned forward on his knees and peeked over the rim of the bowl.

"Hey. Would you look at this?"

Rose and Lucy looked over his shoulder. The stones in the bowl had divided themselves into three groups. Two pebbles were off to one side, four other pebbles made a group opposite the first two, and all other stones were heaped in another pile.

"This must be the score: four to two," James said.

"Or else two to four," said Lucy.

"It's the same thing," James said. "Oh, rats!" He clapped his hand to his head in exasperation. "I forgot to ask which score is which!"

Rose's turn came last. She felt a little nervous. She could ask the oracle something as trivial as whether she would get the shoes she wanted for school next fall. She could ask something as important as what she would be when she grew up. She could ask about Grandma Foley, only it made her feel uneasy putting Grandma Foley's fate in the hands of Gabriella. She wanted something that mattered, but not too much. Finally the question came to her. She spread out her gift, a doll scarf she had made long ago for another doll. It was cut from plaid cloth and had gilt threads, and she had made fringes on both ends.

"O Oracle, beautiful as you are, may I ask my question?"

YOU MAY.

"Will I ever go back to the island and see Ashley?"

YOU WILL.

Right then, Rose thought she could smell the sand and the salt spray again, and she could almost hear the sea gulls crying and children talking over the sound of the waves.

"Thank you," she whispered.

They all waited motionless for a few moments, to be respectful. Then Rose crawled slowly out of the leafy cave and stood up in the hot sunshine. Part of a tune, a twirl of melody, seemed to be coming from Mr. Edgar's apartment. Rose had forgotten all about him. She picked up the picnic blanket from beneath the cherry tree, spread it in the sun, and stretched out on it. Soon she was fast asleep.

The next day Lucy said she couldn't think of any more questions. "Maybe I can ask about Mom again."

"I don't think we should pester the oracle," said Rose. "Why don't you go ahead, James."

"Okay. I've got something." James placed his offering before Gabriella: a pair of doll shoes fastened with pearl buttons. "O Oracle, the greatest ever, can I ask my question?"

I AM LISTENING.

"Will I ever go off the high board this summer?"

WHEN YOU HAVE THE COURAGE.

"Does that mean you will?" asked Lucy.

"I'm not sure," James said.

"I don't want to take another turn yet," said Rose. "We ought to give the oracle a rest. We don't want her to wear out. You can take Gabby in now, Lucy."

Lucy wrapped Gabriella in a snow-white dishtowel (Rose had insisted that it be snow-white, even though that wasn't in the books) and carried her out of the shrine and up to the third-floor bedroom. Lucy was in charge of taking care of Gabby when the oracle wasn't predicting. "We must keep her out of sight," Rose had said. "And I'm afraid you can't play baby with her anymore, Luce." That was all right; Lucy didn't even feel like playing baby. She placed Gabby on a chair and tiptoed away.

On Wednesday morning Rose sat on the curb beside the driveway and stared at the crab grass that had forced its way up through the cracks in the cement. Today she was definitely going to take a turn, but it was still hard to decide what to ask. Should she ask something enormous? Will the sun ever burn out? Will the world come to an end? Or should she ask something infinitely small, such as the fate of an insect. An ant struggled across a sandy crack right before her eyes. If she wanted to, she could ask the oracle what would become of that particular ant. The oracle could say whether the ant would find a bit of sugar to eat, whether its nest would be safe for the summer. Rose could ask anything and everything. If the oracle lasted long enough—and why wouldn't it?—she could ask every time she went out whether anything dangerous was going to happen to her. That would take care of her parents' worries once and for all. If the oracle said no, then she would go on about her business. If the oracle said yes, that something bad was going to happen, then Rose could just stay home. But wait a minute. If the oracle always told the truth, and what she said always happened, then Rose couldn't stay home to avoid the danger. If she stayed home, the dangerous thing would happen to her there. So what was the use of knowing, anyhow? It would only make you nervous.

It might be more interesting to ask what was going to happen to someone else. It might be fun, in fact, to know another person's future. She would ask the oracle about Cindy. She would ask who Cindy was going to marry.

She got to her feet and darted up the back steps. "You guys ready?" she said, sticking her head around the back door and looking into the kitchen.

Lucy and James were sitting at the kitchen table, reading comic books. "What do you mean, are we ready?" said James, getting to his feet. Lucy pulled Gabriella out from under the table, and the three children started across the yard.

Rose had taken the teapot from the doll's tea set to give to Gabby as her offering this morning. They arranged themselves in a semicircle. "O Gabriella, I have a question to ask," Rose said.

I AM LISTENING.

"I want to know who our baby-sitter will marry."

There were clicks and whirring noises. The reply came: A BOATMAN.

"That must be Ron, over at the pond!" Rose clapped her hands. "Thank you, Gabby." It made her laugh.

"Are you going to tell Cindy?" asked Lucy.

"Sure. Or maybe I'll make her guess."

"That isn't very nice," said Lucy.

"We ought to forget this little stuff," said James. "It's a waste to ask silly questions."

"Getting married isn't silly," said Rose.

"Yeah, but it's not you that's getting married. You're just being nosy."

"I am not! What should I ask her then?"

"Something about your own fate. The characters in those books we were reading ask about what's going to happen to them."

"But they all had real fates. They didn't have plain old lives like ours. If we were them, we'd be striding across foreign lands, tricking monsters into cages, marrying kings and queens, turning into trees, and things like that. If I ask the oracle what my fate will be, she'll probably say 'Nothing.' "

"She probably won't," James replied.

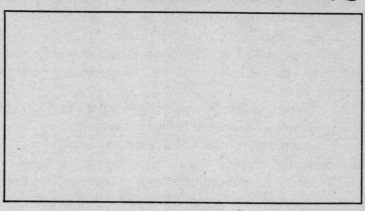

CHAPTER 13

That night Rose was setting the table when the phone rang. "It's for you, Lucy—again," she called. "Who keeps calling you?" This was the third day in a row.

"Just someone," said Lucy, picking up the receiver.

"You can talk for a minute, but that's all. We're about to eat," said their father. "And please ask your friend, after this, not to call at six o'clock."

"It's nearly seven, Daddy," said Rose.

Mr. Wilson was still trying to cook the children's favorite meals, but he had to scurry around to do it when he came home from work. Every day supper got a little later.

Lucy stretched the telephone cord around the corner into the hall so Rose and her father couldn't hear. Rose had measured out a fistful of spaghetti and put it into an enormous pot of boiling water. Homemade meatballs were sizzling in a frying pan. Their delicious onion-and-garlic smell was making Rose's knees wobble. Her father had grated the cheese, and now he was shaking up the jar of salad dressing.

"Lucy!" he called. "You have to hang up!"

Lucy reappeared and stood on tiptoe to replace the receiver on the wall phone. "Yum!" she exclaimed, seeing the stove.

Mr. Wilson added the meatballs to a pot of bubbling tomato sauce. In a moment he had drained the spaghetti, sending up clouds of steam. When the steam had cleared, he poured the slippery strands into a big dish and put it on the table. Rose and Lucy brought over the bowl of sauce, the salad, and glasses of milk. Lucy was twisting the spaghetti strands around her fork even before she had sat completely down.

"Daddy," she began, between slurps, "can I have someone over to play? Tomorrow? Just because James and Rose can't, there's no reason why I can't. I didn't run away."

"That's true," Mr. Wilson agreed. "All right. You can have a playmate."

Lucy finished her supper before anyone else. "I'm going to call her now," she said, excusing herself. She went down the hall into her parents' bedroom and shut the door. A moment later she reappeared. "Daddy? I can't dial."

"Mom always makes the arrangements for Lucy," said Rose.

"The arrangements?"

"If Lucy's inviting someone over here, you have to talk to the mother."

Mr. Wilson pushed back his chair and went into the bedroom. In a moment he and Lucy came back into the kitchen. Lucy was grinning.

"That was easy," said their father. "Now I'm going to call your mother, if we can keep the line free! Who wants to talk first?"

"I will," said Lucy.

"How about you, Rose?"

"I'll say hello."

Her father gave her an odd look. "I'm sure your mother is looking forward to talking to both of you," he said in a puzzled voice.

She couldn't tell him that her mother seemed much farther away than Iowa. And she wanted her to stay there for a while. When she took the telephone from Lucy, she didn't know what to say.

"I miss you," said her mother.

"That's good," said Rose.

"Are you keeping busy?"

"Pretty busy. Here's Daddy."

"We're doing fine, don't you worry," her father explained. "She's just missing you, that's all."

Rose didn't bother to correct him.

Rose was late getting up the next day, and late pulling on her clothes, late eating her breakfast toast, late putting her dishes in the sink. She didn't see Lucy anywhere, or James either.

"Where's James?" she asked, looking around.

"He's coming in a while," said Cindy. "For some reason he picked this morning to go through all his stuff.

Everything in his top drawers is all over his bed. He said he was looking for a key chain. Want me to do your braids?"

I know who you're going to marry, Rose wanted to say. She was dying to see the look on Cindy's face.

"Sure, thanks," she said instead. She loved the feeling of Cindy's brushing her hair. It didn't hurt when she brushed out the snarls, and, because Rose had curly hair, there always were snarls.

"Straight hair gets snarls, too," said Cindy to make her feel better. The comb carved a smooth part all the way from Rose's forehead to the nape of her neck. Rose held one side of her hair while Cindy brushed the other half until the comb slid smoothly through it from scalp to curly tips.

"How would you like it if I told you who you were going to marry?" Rose said.

"Depends on who it is!" laughed Cindy.

"No, seriously."

"Seriously, I wish I had hair like yours," said Cindy, twining her fingers rapidly as she braided three long locks of hair. "Everybody wants curly hair."

"Except the people who have it," said Rose. "I wish my hair were as straight as a piece of string."

"I wouldn't have half as much fun with it then."

Two neat and shining braids now hung down to Rose's shoulder blades. She already felt cooler.

"Wouldn't you like to know who your husband will be?" Rose persisted.

"Actually, no!" Cindy went along with what she thought was a joke. "I love surprises."

"I bet I can tell you."

"I bet you can't."

"Can I go see how I look?"

"One sec. Just let me put in these." Cindy rummaged in her straw bag, turning over bottles of nail polish, thin tubes of eyeliner, and a fat, packed wallet, and pulled out from the bottom two gold barrettes that had tiny star stickers pasted on them. She fastened a barrette on each side of Rose's face, so that they swept her hair up. "How's that?"

Rose skipped to the dining-room mirror and smiled at herself. "I wish my mom could do this," Rose said. "She wants me to get my hair cut."

"Long hair's a lot of work," said Cindy diplomatically. She shook her own flawless fall of blond hair.

"When Mom does my braids, one's always higher than the other."

"Pretty soon you can learn to do your own," said Cindy.

"You're going to marry Ron," Rose blurted out.

"Rose Wilson! Will you mind your own business!" Cindy sounded really irritated, and she left the kitchen. Rose fixed herself another piece of toast, sprinkled it with cinnamon sugar, and drifted onto the back porch. She laughed a little. It was fun telling other people something that they didn't know about themselves, even when they didn't believe you. So what if Cindy didn't like it.

She sat down on the top step to finish her toast. She loved sinking her teeth into the grainy layer of sugar on top of the hot, buttery, crisp outside, and then biting through to the soft inside. After the last bite she yawned strenuously, so that her ears popped. When they had stopped popping, she heard voices coming from the bush. She started across the yard at top speed. She stooped over and peered down the entrance to the green cave. Gabby was sitting on her tripod, and kneeling before her were Lucy and Megan Russell.

Rose scrambled through the tunnel. "What are you doing?" she half shouted, trying to soften her voice partway through the shout, so that she wouldn't sound so frantic.

"Oh! You scared me!" squawked Megan, as Rose elbowed her way in.

"Daddy said I could have a friend," Lucy began. "And Megan kept asking me to invite her over to see the shrine."

"Now you've seen it," said Rose to Megan. "Now it's time to go."

"But I was going to show her Gabby. She wants to hear Gabby tell the future. She's never had a chance to see an oracle before."

"It's not time to ask Gabby anything now," said Rose. "She has to rest in-between questions or she'll wear out. Besides, I hate to disappoint you, Megan, but it's only a game. You'd have to pretend to hear her, you know."

"I knew it," said Megan. "I knew you'd make up some excuse."

"Listen. This is all she says." Rose picked the doll up and tilted her. "Hi-ya!" said the voice box.

"See?"

"Ma-ma!" said the voice box.

"Lucy told me she tells the future," Megan said. "Lucy says you give her presents, and she tells the future. Only you can't always understand what she says."

"Oh, Lucy always says something," said Rose.

"You made it all up!" Megan said to Lucy in dismay.

"I did not!" said Lucy. "Let me show you."

"Lucy! No! Don't you remember what we said?"

"But you and James always get her. I hardly ever have a chance."

"But you don't need a chance!"

"Who says I don't?"

"I do. I'm older than you."

"I want it."

"No."

"It's my doll."

"I don't care." Rose held Gabby tightly, twisting around so she was out of Lucy's reach.

"Rose! I'm going to tell! I'm going to tell Daddy tonight!"

"Go ahead!"

"Oh, forget it," Megan said. She crawled out of the tunnel and went home.

Well, at least we're rid of her, thought Rose. "We've got to keep Gabby a secret, can't you remember that?" she snapped at Lucy.

"You're not the total boss of her," said Lucy.

"I never said I was." Rose realized she was still holding Gabby out of Lucy's reach. "Here, take her! You ought to be glad I came along in time to keep her away from Megan!" Rose shoved Gabby into Lucy's hands and flounced out of the shrine as best she could while crawling on her hands and knees. Then, standing in the sun in the open yard, she began to wonder about what she had done. Hadn't Mr. Edgar warned them about that? He had said possessing the oracle could make people turn

nasty. But Mr. Edgar meant other people. He didn't
mean them.

Lucy walked past Rose without looking back. She was
holding Gabby tightly, and Rose could see she had been
crying.

Lucy stayed away from Rose the rest of that day, but
Rose didn't care, because she was thinking hard. She was
deciding what her first big question to the oracle
should be.

"What are you going to ask next time?" she said to
James. He had carried a kitchen chair over from his
house, and now, after spreading out newspapers on the
driveway, he was giving it a coat of yellow paint. His
mother had told him he had to spend some of his time
usefully.

"I'm not telling what," he said.

"Something about your fate?"

"I don't want to say until I ask it."

"Okay. I don't care."

Rose dug a path through the grass with her heel, rubbing it back and forth. "When are you going to ask it?"

"Probably tomorrow."

James looked as if he was in a bad mood when he walked
over with Cindy the next morning. The three children
drifted toward their daily gathering place in the backyard. When they were well away from the kitchen, James
said, "I've brought a big present today."

"What for?" asked Rose.

"I want to make sure I get a good answer."

"What'd you bring?"

"A silver key chain."

"Real silver?"

"Real silver. It's got my initials on the tag. The tag's silver, too. See? My father gave it to me. I'm not supposed to use it till I'm older."

"But if you give it to the oracle, you might not have it when you're older."

"If you want an important answer, you can't just give her a piece of plastic."

"I guess not." Rose was starting to feel nervous, and she could tell James was, too. She had a vague idea what he was going to ask, and she was afraid of what Gabriella might answer.

Before filing into the cave, they looked around the yard carefully to make sure there were no unannounced visitors. They saw no one. James went in first and laid the silver key chain in front of Gabriella's tripod. Lucy put Gabriella into position, and James motioned the two girls back.

"O Gabriella, who knows everything about what is to come, will you hear my question?"

They sensed energy gathering in the leafy cave. Rose wished James would hurry up and get this over with.

YOU MAY ASK YOUR QUESTION, said the melodious voice.

"What I want to know is, is my father coming to see me?"

NO, came the abrupt answer.

There was a ghastly silence. Rose saw James swallow. "Oh," he said limply. Color rose in his neck and up his cheeks. He opened his mouth, as if he wanted to say something else, and then closed his lips without saying it.

Rose's stomach churned.

"I'm getting out of here," James said, knocking her sideways as he pushed past and scrambled out the tunnel. Rose looked after him. He stood with his back to the cave for a minute, and when he turned around his face was white and rigid. "Damn your stupid oracle," he hissed at Rose and ran toward the house.

Rose's ears were pounding and ringing. She wanted to kick Gabby. "What did you have to say that for?" she said.

HE MUST ASK THE RIGHT QUESTION, said the oracle, her voice trailing away as though she were losing interest.

"Poor James," whispered Lucy.

BEWARE OF HIM WITH A SCAR, the oracle added.

For the rest of the day, James wouldn't even go near the green cave. Rose didn't dare bring up the subject of the oracle, and Lucy didn't talk to either one of them. James sat slouched down on the end of his spine watching television—quiz shows, cartoons, movies. When Cindy tried to get him to go outside and paint another chair, he was so cross and mean that she let him alone.

Today, however, was the day Rose had chosen to ask her first big question. After the answer James got, she almost changed her mind. She decided she didn't want an audience.

"You better not come out with me this time," she said to Lucy, tucking Gabby under her arm. "You might get upset if the oracle gives an answer you don't want to hear." Rose could see from Lucy's expression that her sister was about to protest, so she went out quickly.

For her present Rose had picked out one handkerchief from a set her grandmother had given her. Each of the twelve linen handkerchiefs was a different brilliant color. She had chosen the turquoise one to give to Gabby. It was her favorite.

Rose put the folded handkerchief in front of Gabby and sat back. It felt peculiar to be doing this without Lucy and James. She had been thinking of different ways to put the question, and each time she had tried out a wording in her head, she had imagined the answer that would come. The answer was never quite right, so she kept changing the question. Now she made herself ask it right away: "O Oracle, who knows everything, tell me. Is my grandmother going to die?" There. The words were out.

ONLY THE SOUL IS IMMORTAL.

Rose felt a flash of anger. She wanted a real answer, not some old saying. "But is she going to die now? While she's sick?"

SHE WILL NEVER BE WELL. HER REMAINING DAYS WILL BE SPENT WITH HER FAVORITE COMPANION.

Grandma Foley was already spending them with a favorite companion. That was Rose's mother.

"Thanks," said Rose. "For nothing," she added bitterly. It was no use asking "How many days?" or something like that. Gabby would just have some other roundabout answer to give. And what difference did it make? Then Rose did something that shocked even her. She picked up the doll and threw her as hard as she could to the ground. The doll bounced, and the voice box squawked and squealed. Rose had known the doll wouldn't break. She picked her up after a moment and set her back on the tripod. "What do you care what happens to me, or to any of us?" she said angrily.

IT IS NOT MY BUSINESS TO CARE, said the oracle. YOU ARE ANGRY BECAUSE YOU ARE DISTRESSED.

"You don't have to be an oracle to know that!" Rose exclaimed. "How would you like it if somebody told you what your future was going to be, and you didn't care for it, but you were stuck knowing it? How would you like it? Here's a question for you, Mrs. Oracle. What's *your* future?" She was on the verge of grabbing up the doll and hurling her entirely out of the cave.

I HAVE A FUTURE, said the oracle, her voice as clear and calm as ever. I WILL RETURN TO MY BIRTHPLACE. AFTER THREE COINS FALL, A PERILOUS JOURNEY WILL BRING ME TO A THRESHOLD WHERE MY GUARDIAN WILL RELINQUISH ME. THEN I SHALL GO HOME.

Rose heard the words, but anger was still sparking in her head, and she didn't think about what the words meant.

"I'm sorry I threw you down," Rose said mechanically. It wasn't much of an apology. Gabby's face was vacant now, anyway. Rose brushed the new smudges from the doll's cheeks, tucked her under her arm, and crept out into the sunshine.

"Hey, what'd she say to you?" James asked her when she walked into the house. He looked up, but didn't move from his snail-like coil on the low couch.

"Nothing I wanted to hear," said Rose, and she headed for her room.

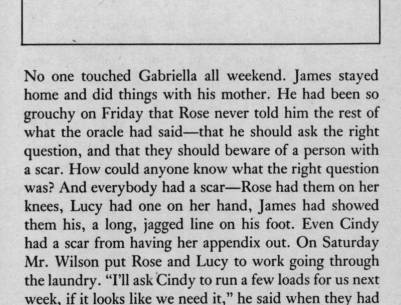

CHAPTER 14

No one touched Gabriella all weekend. James stayed home and did things with his mother. He had been so grouchy on Friday that Rose never told him the rest of what the oracle had said—that he should ask the right question, and that they should beware of a person with a scar. How could anyone know what the right question was? And everybody had a scar—Rose had them on her knees, Lucy had one on her hand, James had showed them his, a long, jagged line on his foot. Even Cindy had a scar from having her appendix out. On Saturday Mr. Wilson put Rose and Lucy to work going through the laundry. "I'll ask Cindy to run a few loads for us next week, if it looks like we need it," he said when they had sorted out the dirty clothes. There were ten heaps in a big circle on the floor around the dining-room table.

"It looks like we need it," Lucy nodded.

"We don't mind wearing dirty shorts," said Rose. She

had worn the same pair all week, and she was wearing them now.

"Let's take these piles down to the basement," said Mr. Wilson. "At least they'll be out of sight."

He talked to their mother on Sunday. Grandma was in a "precarious state," he reported to the children. He didn't know when their mother would come home. It would probably be in another week, but she might have to go back again. She wasn't sure Grandma even knew she was there.

"I want another turn," James announced on Monday. They were sitting on the grass eating doughnuts. Cindy had stopped at Dunkin' Donuts on Center Street and brought them all a breakfast surprise. She herself refused to take one, though, because she said doughnuts didn't have the right nutrients.

"Are you going to ask Gabby the same thing?" asked Rose.

"Nope. Something else. You'll see."

Rose licked the powdered sugar from her fingers, crumpled the empty doughnut bag into a ball, and threw it into a trash can. She was the last to crawl into the cave. She wondered later whether things would have turned out differently if she had been the first into the cave, and so had seen that James was going to drop three quarters onto the carpet. From the entrance she saw when he, not even waiting for her, let them fall from his fingers and said, "O Oracle, you incredible doll who knows the future, will you hear my question?"

If she had somehow changed the three coins—told him

to put down two or four, for instance—maybe the inevitable might have been put off. But as it was, three coins fell.

I AM LISTENING, said Gabby.

"I want to know what the winning lottery number will be this week," said James.

"James!" whispered Rose. They had never tried to use the oracle to win money.

THE STONES SPEAK, said the oracle. The plastic dish jiggled, as if an invisible hand had shaken it. The stones rattled, and then there was silence.

"Thank you very much," said James smugly. He sat unmoving for several moments, to show respect. Then he crawled forward and peeked into the bowl. Lucy crept up behind him to see.

"Oh, look! They're in lots of little bunches," she said.

James reached into his back pocket and brought out a piece of paper and a stub of a pencil.

"Yee-yee! Ai-ai-woo-woo-woo!" Bloodcurdling screams came from the tunnel. Rose looked toward the entrance, and there, hunched over and grinning like barbarians, were Charlie and Megan, and behind them two boys Rose had never seen before. They came crashing through the leaves.

"So what have you got in here?" leered Charlie. "Some kind of fortune-telling booth? Who are you, the great guru?"

"Go away!" Lucy screamed.

The four invaders were into the cave in a flash. Megan headed straight for the little figure of Gabby, perched on her stool. Lucy reached over and snatched up Gabby.

"Grab the doll!" cried Charlie, scrambling in after Megan. He knocked over the plastic dish. The pebbles scattered everywhere.

"You stupid!" cried James. Charlie began throwing the presents around.

There was a terrible scuffle. Charlie and his two friends were hitting and pushing James and laughing. Rose got thrown down into the branches, and between flailing knees and elbows she saw Megan biting Lucy's arm. Lucy yelped and let go of the doll. Megan grabbed it and scuttled out, clutching it to her stomach.

"She's got her! She's getting away with her! James, quick! Lucy! Grab her!"

But the two boys were sitting on James, while he rolled back and forth and tried to kick them off.

Lucy crawled out of the cave on her own, crying. "I'm getting Cindy!" Rose heard her say.

"James! Get Megan!" Rose yelled, but it was too late. The boy who had been tackling Rose suddenly let go of her and crawled as fast as he could out of the tunnel. Rose scrabbled after him. He made it out of the cave and yelled to Charlie and the other boy, who still had James pinned to the ground in the cave. The two boys scrambled out onto the grass.

"Let's go!"

"Have you got it?"

"Put it in the bag!"

Rose saw Charlie sling a plastic drawstring bag over his shoulder. It said "Evans Shoes" on the side, and there was something lumpy in it. The three boys jumped for their bikes, running alongside and hopping and throwing their legs over. Megan stood at the head of the driveway in a panic, swiping at one pedal with her foot. It spun uselessly. "The gears are out!" she yelled. Rose and James caught up to her. James grabbed her arm.

"Where is it? You sneak! You bunch of cheating sneaks!"

"You stole it!" cried Rose. "You better give it back. You better, Megan."

"Hey, what's all the fuss?" asked Cindy, appearing at the back door with her arm around Lucy's shoulder. "What's going on?"

"It was Charlie's idea," Megan said to Rose.

The three boys were long gone.

"I'm telling your mother," said Rose. "She'll make you give it back."

"Tell her," Megan defiantly. "She'll never believe you."

"Wait a minute," said Cindy. "I asked what's going on. Lucy says you bit her, Megan. Look at this place on her arm."

Lucy, hiccupping and taking deep breaths, held out her arm. A large circular red welt showed right above her wrist.

"We played a joke on them," said Megan. "It wasn't a bad joke. We just wanted to make some excitement. We thought they might be getting bored having to stay home. I think one of those boys bit her."

"You did!" said Lucy. "And you told me you would be my friend."

"You liar," said Rose to Megan, at the same moment.

"What was this joke?" asked Cindy.

"Charlie had the idea of kidnapping Lucy's doll. Doll-napping. We were just playing a game with it, though. He won't hurt it."

"You ganged up on Lucy?" said Cindy.

"Sort of. We were pretending to be Indians, and we raided the ranch and took a captive."

"Biting isn't part of a joke," said Cindy.

Megan was silent. "Charlie'll bring it back," she said, finally. "He was meaning to do that from the very start."

"All right, then," said Cindy. "And I don't know who bit Lucy, but if it ever happens again, I'll personally punish that person. And I don't mean scolding." She looked right at Megan, and then she and Lucy went back in.

"It's all your fault," Megan said to Rose. "If you'd ever let someone else see your stuff, we wouldn't've had to get this idea."

"Oh, right, it's our fault," said Rose.

"I'm going home now," said Megan. "My mom's taking me shopping this afternoon," she added.

"You bring that doll back, or else," said James.

"You'll get your stupid doll," said Megan. She started down the driveway, ducking her head. As she turned the corner onto the sidewalk, she glanced back up at them, and Rose saw a sly smile on her face, as if she couldn't help laughing. Then she turned her head away so that Rose couldn't see her expression.

Rose stood very still, and in the stillness she heard a paper bag rattling against a tree trunk, an airplane droning overhead, someone's high heels clicking on the pavement. Her ears rang, and her heart beat through the ringing.

"She's gone," she said in a whisper. She looked over at James. "Gabby's gone. We should have been watching. For someone with a scar."

"For who?"

"After you left the cave last time, the oracle said to beware of him with a scar. But we all have scars."

"They've got her now. They wrecked everything, too," said James. "And I didn't get the number."

Rose crossed the yard and crawled through the tunnel into the bush. It was wrecked, all right. Everything was all over the place: their presents scattered, the plastic dish kicked aside, the smooth brown stones strewn everywhere. One leg of the tripod was knocked crooked. The matted leaves and twigs were torn up and tracked across the carpet. Not only was Gabby herself gone, but the spirit of the place was gone, too. Rose felt that distinctly among the dirty toys and ripped leaves.

"Do you think they'll bring her back?" asked Rose.

"Why would they? If they went this far, to raid the shrine and steal her, why would they bring her back?"

"But Cindy knows they took her. And we can tell Anita. She'll make them bring her back."

"She might, or she might not. You can't count on mothers. You can't tell Anita what Gabby really is, anyway. She'd never believe you if you told her the truth."

"But Anita isn't that mean. If we tell her it's Lucy's special birthday doll."

"You can't count on it, Rose. Those guys'll say they haven't got it, or they gave it back."

"Then what are we going to do?"

"Beats me. Steal it back?"

"You mean break into their house?" Rose asked with a gasp.

"Sure."

"Oh, yeah, really."

Well, what do you suggest?"

"Nothing. Nothing at all."

"Well, Rose, as you once said to me, don't give up yet. I want that number. I want another turn, and I want that number."

CHAPTER 15

"Not that doll again!" said Mr. Wilson.

"But Daddy," wailed Lucy. "They took it. We had this game to keep ourselves busy, and we were in the bushes, and they snuck up. And I want it. Mama bought it for me. It was especially for me for my birthday!" Lucy's misery cranked her voice higher and higher.

"Lucy, here, sit on my lap." Mr. Wilson put down his briefcase, sat down in a chair, and folded Lucy into his arms. "First, we'll calm down."

"Please call Anita, Dad. Megan bit Lucy on the arm, too. It's still red. Look at it."

"There, there." Mr. Wilson hugged Lucy comfortingly. Suddenly Rose wanted to be hugged, too. "I will call her. Let's see your arm."

The mark from the bite had faded, but it was still red. Lucy and Rose waited by the telephone.

"Hello, Anita? George Wilson here. . . . Fine,

thanks. . . . I hear from her every day, but her mother is not doing well. . . . Yes, I'll tell her. I have to ask you about something else. Our girls say your two kids and a couple of their friends had a fight with them today. . . . That's right. About a doll. They're very upset about it. They say Charlie and Megan took Lucy's new doll—some sort of Indian raid—and they want it back. It was a birthday present, and Lucy's very attached to it. . . . Oh, you've heard about it? . . . They did? . . . She does?—They're bringing it back," he whispered to Rose and Lucy—"That should take care of it. Except one other thing. Someone bit Lucy during the fight. She thinks it was Megan. . . . I saw the mark, yes. You're sure it can't have been Megan? She's sure it was. In any case, in our house biting is a serious matter. If it happens again, our children won't be allowed to play with yours."

Rose and Lucy silently clapped their hands.

"Tomorrow morning will be fine. I won't be here, of course, but the sitter will be. Thanks, Anita. Good-by, then."

He turned to the girls. "Anita says it was a severe case of envy. She went out today and bought Megan a talking doll, too. So now she has one, and she'll return yours tomorrow. There now. Starting to feel better?"

Rose and Lucy both hugged their father at once.

Sure enough, on Tuesday morning the front doorbell rang. Rose and Lucy raced to answer it. Charlie and Megan stood at the doorstep. Anita was watching them from her car. She waved to Rose and Lucy. Megan was holding a flannel bundle.

"We brought her back," she said.

"We're supposed to apologize," Charlie grunted.

"Our mom made us wash the clothes to make you feel better. And we're sorry about the shrine"—she giggled—"or whatever it was. Can't you fix it back up?"

"Just give her here," Rose said. She opened the screen door a crack and stuck her hand through. Megan handed over the bundle.

"Bye-bye," said Megan instantly, and she and Charlie ran back to their car. Anita waved again, as if to say "Well, that's settled," and the Russells drove away.

Rose and Lucy unwrapped the doll blanket and looked inside.

"It's not her!" they said together.

It was the same kind of doll, they explained to Cindy, but it wasn't *the* one. The face was the same, the hair was the same, the dress was the same, but it was not Gabby. The voice box said all the same things, even in the same tinny voice: "Mama," "Hiccup," and all the rest. "But she looks new," said Lucy. "She smells new."

Cindy turned the doll over and looked at it from all angles. "What's the difference?" she said. "Looks to me like you lucked out. You got a brand-new doll instead of the old one."

"But I want the old one," said Lucy. "It was my favorite. And my mother gave it to me!"

"I know, sweetie," said Cindy. "When it's your best doll, that's the very one you have to have. I suppose they did this just to be mean. What weirdos."

"Their mother buys them anything they want," said

Rose. "But she doesn't cheat. She wouldn't have let them do this if she knew. They must have fooled her somehow."

"You could have fooled me," said Cindy.

"Will you call her up and tell her to make them bring it back?" asked Lucy. "Our mom would do that."

"Let me think about it," said Cindy.

"But we have to have it," Rose blurted out. She realized then that Cindy was afraid to call Anita. Cindy was only a baby-sitter, after all, and Anita was one of the main-stream mothers.

"I'm not sure what the best way to do this is," was all Cindy would say.

"Look, he said if we had any problems with the doll to come back to him," Rose argued. James tossed his closed Swiss Army knife up in the air, caught it, tossed it again, caught it. They were sitting on the patio. Lucy was inside helping Cindy bake a cake.

"I don't trust that guy," he said.

"What do you think the Russells are doing with Gabby? Suppose they catch on to what she is?" Rose could picture it: Gabby beginning to talk; Charlie and Megan half-hearing the words and laughing at them; the two of them making sense out of it—and then they would never give her back. They'd get their parents in on it, and pretty soon the Russells would run the world. Or, just as bad, Charlie and Megan might hear Gabby but not recognize what she said and get tired of her and throw her out. Then she really would disappear forever. Rose tried to imagine looking for Gabby while poking through an immense city dump. Or, worse, they probably had a trash compactor. She might already be crushed down to the size of a peanut.

"James, we have to get her back!"

"I know it. I told you the only way I can think of."

"But we'd get caught. It's broad daylight. And I don't know how to break into anybody's house."

"So think of something."

"I'm trying. Dad might call Anita again if we ask him to. But I have a feeling that's not going to do us any good. If only we could trick them into giving her back. I know. How about a fake recall letter? My parents got one the other day. It said to send back our waffle iron because the dial might break off."

"It'd never work."

"Maybe a threatening phone call? Threaten to steal their bikes if they don't trade dolls?"

"You'd have to have a grown-up's voice. I can't picture your dad doing that."

"We could offer a reward." But Rose knew she didn't have much to offer, certainly nothing that the Russells didn't already have in dozens. "I still think we ought to go see if Mr. Edgar has any ideas." The thought of Mr. Edgar gave Rose a queasy feeling. But if it was a choice between the queasy feeling and losing Gabby, Rose would put up with the queasy feeling. Then she thought of the trick.

"Did you get her back?" asked their father cheerfully when he came in from work.

"They gave us the wrong one," said Rose. "Look."

Lucy handed the fake Gabriella to her father with a look of distaste. Everything about this doll was bright and shiny and crisp. "Waa-waa-waa," it cried. Mr. Wilson sighed and frowned.

"I want my real one," said Lucy. "Dad, will you call Anita Russell again?"

Mr. Wilson groaned.

"Mom would do it!" said Lucy. "We baked a cake for you, too."

"Can't this wait until later?" Mr. Wilson asked. "There's supper to get, and I need to take a shower, and I'm expecting someone from the office to come by with some papers, and the living room needs to be picked up before he gets here, and I need to work for a while after you children go to bed. Your doll has had plenty of attention from me lately. She has to wait her turn."

"Can we go upstairs and tell Mr. Edgar about it then?" asked Rose quickly.

"Mr. Edgar? Why him?"

"He's been taking an interest in us lately," Rose invented. "He's a doll expert. We think he likes children after all, don't we, Lucy?"

"Why do we think that?" asked Lucy, beginning to suck her thumb in confusion.

Mr. Wilson scratched his head. "It can't do any harm. He probably likes company. But don't stay long. We'll be eating soon. We'll have the cake," he added.

"Bring the doll, Lucy," Rose said, and she led the way out of the house and around to Mr. Edgar's front door. "Now don't be scared."

"Who's scared?" said Lucy.

Rose pushed the bell. She heard his footsteps on the

front stairs, and then there he was, looking at them and at the doll. "You've come back," he said.

It was the first time Rose had seen him face-to-face since their trip to the museum. She was afraid to look him in the eye, so she stared at the frayed buttonhole in his collar. "You said you'd help us with any problems with the doll. Now we've got problems again."

"That's not the same doll, is it," said Mr. Edgar.

"That's the problem," said Rose. From that moment on, she began to feel better.

"Come up then." Mr. Edgar held the door for them.

Rose had never been in Mr. Edgar's apartment. When she reached the landing, she saw that the rooms had the same shape as those on her family's first floor, only these rooms were crammed with old chairs and tables and sofas. Most of the furniture was draped with pieces of cloth fringed with greenish gold tassels and decorated with faded woven pictures. A large framed photograph hung on the wall over the fireplace.

"Who are these people?" Rose asked. The photograph looked very old. A group of ladies with long hair were standing, laughing, with their arms linked around each other. They appeared to be in a play of some kind. They were wearing costumes made of draperies and tunics, and they had names written on the broad sashes that crossed their costumes: Athena, Artemis, Aphrodite. "Are they the ones who lived here?" Rose asked.

"Exactly," said Mr. Edgar.

"Did you know them?" asked Lucy.

Mr. Edgar smiled and said nothing. He was in his benevolent mood.

The dining room was full of plants—plants on the big

round dining table and on the sideboard and on stands around the edges of the room, next to the windows. On one table Rose saw three large pots with small bushes growing in them. She recognized the bush in the middle by its leaves—smooth ovals, darker green on the underside—and its familiar fragrance.

"Hey, you've got a plant like ours," she said.

"I'm an indoor gardener," said Mr. Edgar. "I've rooted cuttings from many plants in the yard. And from plants growing elsewhere."

"That one is like our special bush." Lucy pointed toward the table.

"You're right. In fact, this is the parent plant. The bush in the yard was grown from a sprig of this one."

"You mean you've lived here all that time?" asked Rose.

"Not quite. The plants have! The plants are older than I am. But let's talk about your problem."

Rose explained.

"This is a serious situation. You are absolutely right—it's dangerous to let the doll stay in other people's hands, particularly those other people. There's one safeguard, though. The oracle needs the plant to inspire her predictions. She can't do anything when she's separated from the greenery."

"Oh, no," Rose groaned. "She's wearing the wreath I made her. Unless it fell off. We haven't any way of knowing if it did."

"Then you must get the doll back. I order you to get it back. You *must!*"

"We want to!" Rose protested. "That's where I thought you could help us. I have this plan, and it might work if you do part of it."

Rose outlined her plan. This was the first Lucy had heard of it, too.

At the end, Mr. Edgar smiled and nodded his head. "Clever. We'll try it. Let's give them an extra day. We'll set it for Friday. By the way, you haven't said anything to your father about your doll, have you? About its special powers?"

"No, I haven't. Say, what's in here?" Rose asked, peering through a half-open door as they went down the hallway. The room that was her father's study on the first floor appeared to be a storeroom in Mr. Edgar's apartment. "What are all these things?"

Mr. Edgar turned on a lamp, and its low light picked out a strange assortment of objects. There were collections of dice and of smooth, sticklike bones that had black marks on them. There was a whole shelf of large, milky-colored glass balls resting in holders. There were decks of cards and boxes of tea. Rose saw three black glass "eight" balls, the kind children buy at the dimestore that are supposed to tell the future but are only toys. She picked one up and shook it. An answer floated up in the window on the bottom. "Certainly so," it read. In the corner a stringed instrument leaned against the wall. It was U-shaped and had seven strings.

"What do you think all these are for?" asked Mr. Edgar.

"I know what they are," Rose said slowly. "They're all things for telling the future."

"That's right. I have made a hobby of collecting devices that tell the future. Divination has always interested me—that word means knowing the future—and I find it amusing to collect objects that people have used to tell their futures."

"So that's why you've been so interested in Gabby," Rose said boldly. "I guess you wish you could collect her!"

"I would love to," said Mr. Edgar. "But the only proper way for me to acquire her would be if you gave her to me."

"Why is that?" Rose frowned.

"I couldn't even buy her from you."

"Why not?"

"It takes more than money to establish possession," said Mr. Edgar. "Just plain money doesn't legitimize it."

"What does that mean?"

"It means you have to need the oracle. Or you have to deserve it because you have struggled for it or fought for it or protected it in some way. Money alone doesn't work."

"But you told us we should destroy it! How come you said that?"

"I wanted to test you. I thought that you would be completely horrified if I said that. If you were true guardians of the oracle and wanted to keep it safe, you would leave as quickly as possible and not come back to me for help unless you really needed it. It was a test of loyalty. And you passed it."

"I thought you were being mean."

"Did you think of trying to destroy it?"

"Not even once." Rose shook her head. "Even if the oracle stopped talking, Lucy would still want to have the doll to play with."

"I am glad to hear you say that. Of course, you might not have been able to destroy it. If you had tried, the spirit of the oracle would probably have escaped and taken up residence elsewhere."

"Maybe it would have come to you!" Rose said brightly. Then she wished she hadn't spoken so fast. Mr. Edgar's old alert look, the one that had scared her so much, was back on his face in an instant, his blue eyes penetrating her glance, freezing her with their intensity. She realized that she had read his mind: She had guessed correctly.

"Or to my dad! Or my mom!" she went on, in the same light voice. Her expression had given her away, though. Everything was getting confusing again, just when she felt Mr. Edgar had turned out to be their friend. "But since we didn't destroy her, we have her still, or, I mean, we will have her, as soon as we get her back. Do you think we will?" she asked, opening her eyes very wide and pretending she was six years old.

"I'm sure I don't know," said Mr. Edgar.

The children left immediately.

CHAPTER · 16

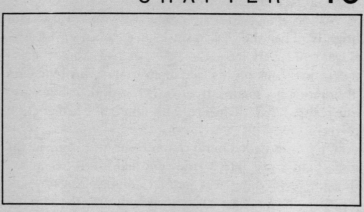

Lucy practiced what she was going to say. She practiced in front of the mirror, she practiced in the closet, she practiced in the backyard all the next day. This was a very important thing that she had to do. It made her feel important to practice, and the more important she felt, the more she knew she *was* important. But she couldn't tell her mother about it. Even when she talked to her mom long-distance on the telephone, she was not supposed to tell. That was what they had made her promise. Not now, and not later, either. Keeping the secret was hard. But she would. She tightened her fists and stared at herself in the mirror and said, "Don't tell." Judging from her reflection, she was sure she wouldn't.

On Thursday morning Lucy packed her bathing suit and towel in her swim bag and went downstairs. Cindy was already in the kitchen, running in place, and Rose was sitting in a patch of sunlight fiddling with her bran flakes. She gave Lucy a smile that was both sneaky and friendly as Cindy bent down to touch her toes.

"Cindy, can you call Anita Russell?" Lucy asked. "She promised my mom she'd take us swimming, and today I want to go, even if Rose can't."

Cindy straightened up, her face flushed red, and began running again. "Sure. Why not? But what about the doll-snatching? You still mad about that?"

"Not so much," said Lucy.

"I don't mind," Rose added. "I can't stand the Russells anyhow."

Lucy ate her breakfast, and Cindy called Anita Russell. Lucy and Rose were holding their breaths during Cindy's conversation. It was all no use if the Russells weren't going swimming.

"Sure thing. I'll have her ready in two shakes," said Cindy. Lucy and Rose could hear Anita's enthusiastic burbling all the way across the room.

At ten minutes of ten, Anita pulled up in front of the Wilsons' house and honked her horn. Lucy had the new Gabriella in one hand and her swimming things in the other.

"Have a good time with the creeps," said Rose.

"Right." Lucy gave her sister a chipper wave and set out. Anita had opened the back car door for her. Lucy got in and fastened her seat belt. The Russells' car was always clean, clean, clean. That was one thing about the Russells. They were tidy.

Lucy settled Gabriella on her lap, making a lot of rustling noises and plumping the doll's arms and legs around so that her voice box talked. Lucy smiled at Megan and Charlie. They were watching her, but they weren't saying anything. Lucy hadn't seen them since the day the Russells delivered the wrong doll. Lucy gave Gabriella a big, show-off hug.

"You're so fond of that doll, aren't you?" said Anita, looking in her rearview mirror.

"It's because she's really special," said Lucy.

"I can see that," said Anita.

"She's even more special than you can see," said Lucy.

"Oh, is she?"

"Yep. Mr. Edgar told me so. He looked at her and said she was one of a kind. I don't know what that means, though, but he said be really careful with her."

"Why is that?" Anita had stopped at a red light, and she turned all the way around to look at Lucy.

"He said there's only a very few like her in the entire world, probably three, and the factory made about a zillion. If you have one of those three special ones, you're really lucky."

"What is it about those three?" asked Anita.

"I can't remember." Lucy shrugged her shoulders and gave Gabriella a little kiss.

"He didn't say, hmm?"

"I think he did, but I forgot!" Lucy giggled.

"That's interesting."

Once they were at the Y, Lucy stuck to the shallow end and dog-paddled back and forth. She dunked her head under once, holding her nose. She had propped up Gabriella where she could see her, on a bench heaped with towels. Anita sat nearby on a dry bench, reading a magazine. Anita never went swimming.

After a few minutes, Lucy climbed out of the pool, padded over to the bench, and wrapped her towel around her shoulders. Then she picked up Gabriella and walked over to Anita's bench and sat down beside her. Anita moved away a few inches, to escape dripping water.

"Want to ask me anything else about my doll?" Lucy said.

Anita laughed. "Like what?"

"You can ask anything!" Lucy said. She and Rose hadn't discussed what to do if Anita wasn't interested.

"What should I ask?"

"What about how valuable Mr. Edgar said it was?"

"He said that? He said it was valuable?"

Lucy nodded. "Hundreds of dollars. He's going to look at as many as he can, everywhere, to find the other ones. The other ones with the special sign."

"He's doing this now?"

"Yep. Starting this Friday. *All day Friday.*" She said this especially loudly. "He's having different people bring their dolls to the museum. And he'll look at them. He's already seen mine, so I don't have to go."

"Do you want to know something?" said Anita. "Maybe your father told you. After that awful trick Megan and Charlie played on you, Megan asked me to get her a Gabriella doll just like yours, and so I did."

Lucy looked down at the doll in her lap. "Really?" she asked, looking at the water in the pool that was slapping up over the rim of the drain.

"After what you've said, I wonder if she might possibly

be one of the three. It's unlikely, but possible."

"It's possible, all right!" Lucy tried not to sound too excited. "You never know," she added, pretending to yawn.

"Friday is tomorrow," said Anita.

"Mm-hmm," said Lucy. She buried her face in Gabriella's stiff curls to hide her smile.

On Friday morning Rose and Lucy woke up early. They were both feeling nervous. Rose heard Mr. Edgar's front door open and close, and she went over to her window to try to catch sight of him. He was going up the sidewalk, carrying a small suitcase and a bulging shopping bag from a department store. He looked like such a small figure from the third-floor window. He was bent and lean, yet he didn't walk like any old person she had ever seen. At times Rose wondered if he were someone in disguise.

"I'm going to ask Dad now," Rose said to Lucy. She hurried down the back stairs and into the kitchen. She could hear the shower running, then being shut off, and in a moment her father opened the bathroom door a crack, so that a cloud of steam poured out.

"'Morning, Daddy," she called through the door.

"'Morning to you," he said back.

"Are you going to work today?"

"Of course I am." The clink of his razor was followed by the swish of water being run into the bathroom sink. "What are you going to do?"

"Not much, I guess."

"How are you and James doing with your mythology project?"

"My what? Oh, that. It's fine. We're nearly done with it."

"What next?"

"We don't know. Uh, Dad?" She hesitated. "Are we still on punishment?"

"Yes!" Her father sounded so decisive Rose's heart sank. He opened the door wider and looked out at her. He was wearing his terry-cloth bathrobe, and half of his face was still covered with shaving cream. He went back to his shaving. Rose came into the bathroom and sat on the edge of the bathtub.

"Can I watch you shave?" she asked.

"Sure." He began carving a clean path through the white foam on his jaw.

"Dad?"

"What is it?" He began to sound annoyed.

Rose let out a long, noisy breath. "I need to ask you something, only I know you'll say no."

"You can try."

"I want to go somewhere today. I need to go."

"Can't it wait?"

"No. It's now or never. Really."

"What is it?"

"I can't tell. I promised I wouldn't. But it isn't anything bad."

"I'd like to say yes, but I can't go back on my decision."

"What if I stay in an extra week to make up for today?"

"That would make it convenient for you, but the whole point of being punished is that it is inconvenient. We hardly ever punish you children, so you aren't used to it."

"I don't want to get used to it."

"You're in charge of that, now, aren't you?"

"You are," said Rose, sounding ruder than she meant to.

Her father didn't say anything, because he was carefully shaving his chin, stretching his jaw to the side so that the razor moved smoothly over it. He rinsed the razor under the faucet. "I'm going to call your mother this morning at work."

"What for?"

"I'm worried. We haven't had any news for two days."

Rose felt a pang of fear. The news he was going to get was probably that Grandma Foley was dying.

Her father rinsed his face and dried it on a towel. "Cindy can think up something for you to do at home. How about baking cookies?"

Cookies. Cookies! When Gabriella at this very moment might be telling Charlie or Megan about Rose's plan. Or she might be lying in the bottom of a closet under a heap of old clothes, and she might not be retrieved for a hundred years if Rose didn't do the retrieving right now.

"Okay," Rose said.

"Okay, what?" asked her father from across the hall. He had already started getting dressed.

"Okay about the cookies."

Mr. Wilson left for work the moment Cindy arrived. James followed Cindy in the door.

"What'd your father say?" he asked Rose, without even saying hi.

"The answer is no," said Rose.

"Uh-oh," said Lucy. She had brought the new Gabriella downstairs and propped her near the back door, ready for Rose.

"The answer to what?" asked Cindy. She slung her straw bag up on the counter and sorted through it, looking for her hairbrush. She brushed all her hair back into a ponytail, wound it around and around her hand, slipped it all into a shining coil, and fastened it in place with three hairpins. She looked beautiful, as usual. Rose suddenly felt very small and unkempt.

"The answer to whether we can get off punishment for one day."

"No go, huh?"

"Nope."

"Where are we on breakfast?" Cindy bustled on. "You've already had it? How about you, Lucy? Want some yogurt? Cheerios?"

"Dad says we should bake cookies today," said Rose.

"Why not?" said Cindy. "That's something you guys can do all by yourselves."

Rose scanned the kitchen bookshelf and pulled down a spiral-bound book called *Fifty Foolproof Cookies*. "I'm going to look for a recipe," she said. "Come on, James." She went out the patio door and sat down on the brick steps. The steps were still cool, since the sun came up on the other side of the house, and there was a good smell of damp earth and honeysuckle around the patio. James sat down beside her. She opened the book to "Martha's Marshmallow Marvels" and said, "We have to get there."

"We went once without asking. We can go twice. I'm not sure I ever want to see that doll again, though," said James.

"One six-ounce package of miniature marshmallows," said Rose, turning around. Behind the screen door Cindy stood with a mug in each hand.

"Have some strawberry-apple juice," she said. "I just bought it yesterday. Can you get the door?"

James opened the screen door and took the mugs.

"Cindy's so nice. It's too bad she can't help us," said Rose, sipping the juice. It was awfully sweet. Suddenly she jumped to her feet. "I've got it! Let's help *her*. Let's offer to help with the groceries." She dashed back into the house. "Cindy! I've got something to ask you. James and I want to do something different today. We're going crazy staying home. So why don't we go up to the grocery store and do the shopping? We need the exercise. It can count as helping you around the house. Come on, please."

Cindy was sweeping some Cheerios into the dustpan. She dumped them into the trash can.

"I don't know what your father would say," she said.

"You don't have to tell him."

"Oh, it sounds all right to me. But just Rose should go. I've got another errand for James later this afternoon. If you go together, that's too much like having fun. You're still under house arrest, you know. So I'll give you some grocery money, Rose, and you can go right now, while it's early." Cindy handed Rose a ten-dollar bill and a piece of scrap paper. "Your father left me a big list. Why don't you write down a few of these things."

Rose's head spun. Between writing "carrots" and "macaroni" and "a cut-up frying chicken," she was trying to remember the route to the museum. The last thing she had counted on was having to go by herself.

"And is this a Cabbage Patch doll?" asked the lady. "No, I see it isn't. Well, it's a cute dolly, even so."

Rose looked away from the woman and down Center Street, willing the streetcar to come, to hurry. "Hi-ya!" said the new Gabriella to the woman, over Rose's shoulder. The woman looked a second time at the doll and moved away. Rose groaned. If only she had stuffed the doll in a bag or wrapped her in a towel to muffle the sound.

Rose had to admit to herself that she was scared. James was going to tell Cindy in half an hour that Rose had not gone to the grocery store, but was off on an important trip. They didn't want Cindy to have a real fright, and this would give Rose enough time to get on the streetcar. Where was she supposed to get off? All she could remember was Boylston, Boylston, Boylston. But hadn't they stayed on past that? She could ask someone. No, she shouldn't talk to strangers. Ask the driver. But she would never understand what he said. For that matter, how did she know which streetcar to get on?

When the trolley did finally pull up at the stop, Rose climbed on fast to keep herself from chickening out. As she jolted along on the streetcar, she found that she could remember each of the places where she had been scared the first time, and so, bit by bit, the way began to seem familiar. When they came to the wall that said "Boylston, Boylston, Boylston," she remembered what James had said to her and how hard it had been to get off at Park Street. Today there weren't so many people crowding her. She stepped off the streetcar and looked for the Red Line Outbound sign. She found that right away. She went down the staircase and along the walkway to the platform, where a train sat waiting. She got off at South

Station and followed the signs to the museum. It was all so ridiculously easy.

She paid her admission at the museum desk with part of the ten dollars Cindy had given her, got her hand stamped, and darted up the staircase. Past the second floor, up to the third floor, down the quiet hallway, through the STAFF ONLY doors—"Hey, there, little girl, are you—" *Swish*, the closing door shut out the sound. She went straight to Mr. Edgar's office. His door was locked. She knocked, waited, knocked again. In a moment he opened it.

"Come in, Rose." On top of Mr. Edgar's desk Rose saw the small suitcase he had been carrying, shut, but with a shirt-sleeve caught in the crack.

"I've been tidying up. I'm going to go on a little trip. A doll-collecting trip. Where's your friend James?"

"He couldn't come."

The suitcase gave Rose an uneasy feeling. Then she glanced at the shopping bag that was standing in the corner. It was stuffed with Gabriellas. "Wow! You got a lot of them," she said.

"A whole dozen," said Mr. Edgar.

It was part of the plan. Mr. Edgar took Rose's fake Gabriella and the others into his workroom. He arranged four of them on his table and put the others on a shelf. All the dolls began speaking at once, their voice boxes set off by his footsteps.

"Where can I wait?" she asked. "I want to listen when they get here."

"You can stand behind this door," he said. "When it's open, no one can see you. And I'll take the Russells directly past you into my workroom."

"You're sure they won't notice me?"

"I'm sure. They'll be paying attention only to me."

"What'll we do if they don't come?"

"They are coming," said Mr. Edgar.

How do you know? Rose started to ask, but decided it was better not to get into that subject.

"In the meantime, you can look around the museum for a few minutes. It's just opened."

"Okay. I'll be back at ten-thirty," said Rose. There were big wall clocks everywhere; she could easily keep track of the time.

As soon as Rose had turned her back on Mr. Edgar, a lump of dread, like a cold marble, formed in her stomach. She didn't want to get too far away. She wanted to get her hands on the old Gabby and personally bring her home. She was not going to entrust that job to Mr. Edgar.

Rose wandered into the dollhouse room, then went on to the computer corner. Already screens were flickering with directions and drawings and arrows. A lot of grownups sat at the terminals or hovered over the shoulders of children and poked at buttons. Rose walked over to the stair railing and looked down. There they were. At the same moment, they looked up at her. She pulled back. Had they seen her? She didn't dare look over the side to check. If they had, they would smell a rat in a moment. Even if they weren't smart enough to have figured out Gabby, they were smart enough to have figured out Rose.

Feet were coming up the stairs, voices by the dozen. Was that Charlie she heard? Rose turned on her heel and pushed her way through the third floor, through the doors, down the corridor, and into the office. "They're coming!" she cried. She tucked herself into the corner and pulled the door across to hide herself. They were right behind her.

"I wonder if he'll remember me," Anita was saying.

"We shouldn't be doing this, Ma," said Charlie. "I had a feeling when I woke up this morning."

"Hello?" Rose heard Anita step over the threshold. She could see the tips of Anita's shoes under the crack. "Oh, Mr. Edgar! I don't know if you remember me. I came in a few weeks ago with my daughter's Morgan doll—an original, if you recall? And today we're here with another one, one that I understand you're interested in."

"Naturally I remember you. Do come in. What's the doll? Not one of the Gabriella dolls? Such an interesting development in Gabriellas." Mr. Edgar's voice was so soothing and slow, he could have calmed a cage of wild lions.

"Yes. That's just what it is. I understand today is Gabriella day. Show him, Meggie."

Rose was dying for a look, but she didn't dare move. She heard a muffled but familiar "Ma-ma!" Was Gabby still wearing the wreath?

"Let's go into my workroom and I'll take a good look." Rose edged to the doorframe and peered around it. Mr. Edgar was getting down all the other identical dolls and placing them on the table. They all began talking at once, a chorus of "Hi-ya!" and "Ma-ma!" and "Uh-oh!" Now he opened the box Anita handed him and took out the real Gabby. Rose could have fainted with relief. It was clear Anita had no idea what it really was. "Ours is a little faded," she said. She plucked out the withered leaves caught in Gabby's hair and dropped them in a wastebasket.

Mr. Edgar, talking all the while, began comparing the dolls' heads and the writing on their backs and the way their joints were constructed. He kept picking the dolls up and putting them down, and his voice was getting more and more hypnotic as he mumbled. Soon even Rose could scarcely remember which was the real Gabby. He directed the Russells' attention to some thick catalogs, open on a stand on the other side of the room. While they were turning the pages and looking at the photographs, he quietly put Gabby into the lineup of Gabriellas on the shelf and put a new Gabriella out under his light. Anita turned back to ask a question. She didn't notice the difference.

Rose nearly let out her breath in a huge sigh but she didn't want to make any noise. She wouldn't feel safe until she had Gabriella in her own hands and was home. Then she and Lucy and James would restore the green cave and start their visits once again. James could try for another lottery number. She could ask what she was going to be when she grew up. Maybe even Lucy would think of something to ask. If everything was running smoothly again before her mother came home, she might not even find out about the oracle.

"And so I'm sorry, but this is not one of the valuable ones," Mr. Edgar was saying. "Though it's a perfectly fine doll." He picked up the new Gabriella and held it out to Megan.

"Hey!" said Charlie, elbowing in for a good look. "That's not the same one. Look! This one isn't ours!"

It sure isn't, thought Rose, and darted out from behind the door.

"Oh, Charlie, don't be silly—" said his mother.

"I can't have made a mistake—" from Mr. Edgar.

"It's not?" Megan was saying.

Rose grabbed Gabby from the row of identical dolls and ran back through Mr. Edgar's office into the corridor. Should she go right or left? Left, toward the door to the rest of the museum.

"Hey! That was Rose!"

"I thought I saw her before!"

Rose held Gabby tightly to her chest. It felt good to have the doll's slight weight in her arms again. She ran for the staircase. They would come after her, she knew they would. She didn't dare turn her head to see. They would be storming down the hall. Would Mr. Edgar be with them? Or would he slow them down? Charlie and Megan were fast, Rose knew that. They were mean, and they were fast. They would expect her to try to get out the front door. So she would have to do something else.

"Chinese Market. Come and Buy," read the first exhibit sign she came to. Rose stepped into a corridor of stalls holding fake fruits and vegetables beneath signs written in Chinese characters. A little boy in shorts and sandals was squeezing the plastic green peppers and throwing them back into the bins. A pregnant lady held her squirming daughter by the wrist: "Lookit, Sheryl! Look at the little shoes, all embroidered! Sheryl, you're not even looking!" Rose grabbed a straw hat from the Chinese clothing stall and put it on her head. She dodged through the stalls and skidded around the corner into a man who was squinting at the Indian Life display. "Would you watch where you're going?" he snapped. He was wearing a tweed jacket and taking notes. "Sorry," Rose said and dived past the stuffed deer into the model wigwam, where it was dark. She sat down on a pile of skins, trying to think. If she stayed here and they looked in and saw her, she would be trapped. There was only one way in and out of the wigwam. She pulled the straw hat down a little further over her face and stuck her head out of the wigwam, looking right and left beneath the brim. So far, so good.

"Gotcha!" said a voice, and a hand grasped at her shoulder. Rose jerked away. Charlie reached across the skin-drying rack and groped for a better hold on her.

"Charles, be careful, you're going to knock that thing over," said Anita. "Oh, look, she's right there!" Rose cut back through the Chinese market and ran for the City Life display, straight to the model manhole. One little boy was already at the edge, afraid to step in. He kept putting one foot on the ladder, then taking it off again.

"Let me show you how," said Rose, shoving him out of the way. She turned around and started down the ladder, hanging on with one hand to the skinny metal rail. She descended deeper and deeper, past the mock sewers and pipes and cables that ran through the layers of street. At the bottom she could still hear the little boy crying. He would hold up the Russells, and that gave her an extra minute. She ran into the model of the old-fashioned Grandparents House. From Grandfather's Cellar, stairs led upward, but they were narrow and jammed with people. Rose darted behind the coalbin in the cellar.

There was no one back here, nothing but some old pickle jars. She was out of sight, safe for the moment. She couldn't crouch there all day, though, and she didn't want to be trapped. Instead of hiding in a corner, she would be better off mingling with the biggest crowd she could find. There was always a mob around the Bubbles display. Rose ran once more.

People were standing around big tubs of soapy water and blowing bubbles with pipes, bubbles as big as their heads, bubbles as tiny as marbles, rows and strings of bubbles. The air was full of globes that glistened and floated and popped into extinction. Some children were making a bubble sheet, a thin film that stretched across a tall frame. As they pulled it larger and larger, people on the other side showed through as strange, bulbous shapes. Rose watched as sheet after sheet was drawn up, six feet tall, stretched and stretched, and then burst. The next time the bubble sheet burst, Rose found herself looking straight through the open space at Mr. Edgar. Behind him stood Charlie and Megan and Anita, all watching an enormous bubble that drifted over their heads. Mr. Edgar's eyes met Rose's, and he pointed to an Exit door, holding his hands in front of his chest, so others didn't see his gesture. Then he pointed his finger upward. Rose understood what he meant. She was gone in an instant, tugging the hat down over her eyebrows, shoving past three fathers carrying back-packed babies. Wham—she was through the exit doors and facing a staircase that went out of sight. Running up a flight of stairs was easier than running down. *Don't trip*, she sent a message to her sandals. As she went up, the museum's air conditioning thinned out and the air grew hotter and dustier. She ran by pulling herself along, grabbing at the banister with one hand. She passed the third-floor doors, marked with a big, painted kindergarten "3." Far below her a door opened and released a burst of noise into the staircase. "I saw her," Megan said. Rose clomped on up, as quietly as the average elephant. At least she was out of sight, hidden by the turns of the stairway.

"Didn't she go in here?" Megan asked.

"I saw her heading for the front doors," said Mr. Edgar.

The noise stopped, as if a radio had been turned off. Rose knew Mr. Edgar had steered them away: She was safe. But where was she? She stood at the top landing of the staircase and faced an unmarked set of swinging doors. She pushed through them.

The doors slapped shut behind her, closing her into darkness and silence. Light came dimly through the small windows in the doors and fell onto a scuffed tile floor. It was some kind of storage room, maybe for old exhibits. Rose stood perfectly still, gasping for breath and trying to see. As if someone were slowly turning up the lights in a theater, one by one large objects appeared in the dark, standing at random in a cavernous room. Over there was a big, white stuffed bird; behind it, other stuffed birds, mostly sea gulls—a feathered army all facing the same direction. Here, leaning against a wall, was a giant checkerboard that was big enough to walk on. To one side, empty animal cages stood stacked on top of each other. Beyond them was a metal clothes rack with a lion costume draped on a hanger. Other clothes crowded behind the rack—a spangled sleeve, a silky shirt. At the far end was a cluster of doll carriages and baby carriages, from tiny to huge. Some crooked child-size tables were scattered around. All the toys were dusty. These weren't the valuable ones, the collectors' items: These were just plain toys, the ones children were allowed to get their hands on. They would probably be put out again someday; someday they would have another turn.

Rose sank down on a beanbag chair. A rip in its seam released a rattle of beans onto the floor. It didn't matter now if she made noise. She wanted to breathe, and she wanted her pulse to stop pounding in her forehead. She was roasting hot, as well. For the first time, Rose took a real look at Gabby. She was the same old Gabby, though her frozen smile and painted eyes were now beginning to fade. Her hair was hopelessly stiffened into points. She looked punk. "You're right in style, Gabs," Rose said, giving the doll a hug. When Gabby was being so terribly oracular, it hadn't seemed right to hug her. But for the moment, she was just Lucy's favorite doll again, showing a few signs of wear. Everything would be all right now. After this, they would always keep Gabby under guard or lock and key. They would always watch the entrance to the green cave. They would have Mr. Edgar tell them everything he knew about the care and keeping of oracles. Gabby was theirs again, now and forever.

The double doors swung open. Mr. Edgar was silhouetted against the lighted staircase

"Rose? Where are you?" he called into the dark room.

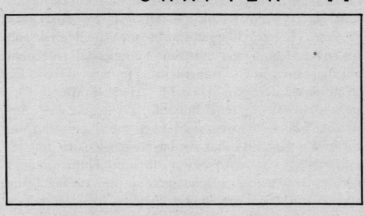

CHAPTER 17

Mr. Edgar came across the dim attic. "Rose? Ah, there you are!" She thought he smiled at her, but his smile chilled rather than warmed her. Rose tightened her grip on the doll. Something wasn't right.

"I want the doll, Rose. You must have guessed."

"I—I haven't guessed anything," Rose stammered. She was nearly as tall as Mr. Edgar, and she had to be at least as strong. She knew she was faster.

"It belongs to me, Rose. You know that."

"It doesn't! It most certainly does not! It was Lucy's birthday present!" Tired as she was, Rose rallied. She had not come all this way only to follow some old crank's orders.

"The voice, the oracle, belongs to me."

It was hard to see in the attic. Rose had to squint to look at Mr. Edgar. The room was dark, but a light was shining in from somewhere, maybe the crack between the doors. Still, it was almost impossible to keep him in focus. It might have been her imagination, but he looked different. He didn't look old. His hair was curly, not straight. He looked larger and broader-shouldered, and his face was no longer thin. His skin glowed; she could tell that, even in the weird light. He had rosy cheeks. "You look different," Rose said. "Are you different?"

"I am always myself," he said. "The oracle was mine for many ages," he went on. "Then she was stolen from me and my family, and we have been looking for her ever since. Our task has been difficult. Human beings no longer believe in oracles, and so they do not listen and do not hear when an oracle speaks."

"Were those ladies your family?" Rose asked suddenly. "The ones you have the picture of? The ones who started the plants?"

"They are. They returned to our home in the Old World, but I stayed to continue searching. You see, it had been foretold that the oracle would return as a child's plaything. You and your sister heard the sacred voice, and your companion James had the courage to recapture the oracle from the serpent. I would like to thank him properly, but now I am going to take the oracle to Delphi, where she belongs. There she may thrive again someday, in another age."

"Why don't we keep her at our house?" Rose argued. "She can thrive with us just as well." She kept looking at Mr. Edgar's face; it seemed extraordinarily handsome, but she couldn't see the whole of it.

"You don't really want to have the sole keeping of an oracle, even if you think you do."

"Sure I do. Just because we made a couple of mistakes doesn't mean we can't do it."

"If you keep the oracle, you will soon become its priestess. You will do nothing but tend the oracle for the rest of your life. You will not want to do anything else. Do you wish to spend the rest of your life in a cave with a doll?"

"No, but do you?" Rose was dazzled and terrified, but she made herself speak up.

"I have helpers who are longing to do just that," he said.

"You can't have her," Rose said stubbornly.

"I will not take her by force. She must be willingly relinquished."

Not by me, thought Rose. But the word tripped in her mind: Hadn't the oracle herself used that word when she was talking about returning to her birthplace?

"We found her," Rose said. "If we hadn't listened to her, nobody would have ever heard her again. And we can go on having her. And asking her the future. For ourselves, for anybody we want. We'll make the cave nice again, too."

"You did find her, and you have saved her, perhaps for all time. But now your job is done. I will bargain with you," he said, smiling. "If you want to know the future, you may ask the oracle now what your entire future will be. We will crush the dead leaves from her wreath, and the perfume will make her speak again. You will know everything—your fate, if you wish, in detail. Everything that will happen to you and to everyone you know will be told, if it pleases you."

Everything? Her whole future—and James's and Lu-cy's? She would know what they would be when they grew up, and whom they would marry, and who their children would be, and whether they would be happy or unhappy. She would know what terrible things were going to happen, and then, of course, she would dread their coming. She would also know what wonderful things were going to happen; but there would never be a surprise, never anything unexpected. If she knew everything that was to come, she would never need to hope for anything. She would know how long her parents were going to live, and how long Grandma Foley would live, too. She would know what she was going to look like when she grew old, and how old she would grow, and—finally—when she would die. All of it would be known.

It didn't sound so good. If she knew everything in her future, she wouldn't feel she was living her life; she would feel as if she was remembering it. She didn't want to give up surprises, or give up hoping for things, and she didn't want to spend a lot of time dreading the future, either. Dreading the dentist every six months was bad enough. She would hate being a priestess in a cave—she had other things in mind to be when she grew up. So there was nothing to do but give up the oracle and go back to being a regular ten-year-old girl, and that would have to be good enough. She knew she was going to feel bad. She had loved being in on something so special.

"You can have the oracle," Rose said. Her voice shook a bit, but she didn't change her mind. "And I don't want to know the future. You can only have the voice box back, though, not the doll. I am going to keep the doll for Lucy. It's really hers. She'll miss it something awful if she doesn't get it back. We can put in a voice box from one of the dolls downstairs."

Rose got up from the beanbag chair and walked over to the double doors so that she could see better. She pushed one open to admit more light, then unzipped Gabby's back and took out the voice-box. She handed it to Mr. Edgar. "Here you are," she said.

He was wreathed in smiles. She could see him clearly now in the hall light, and he hadn't changed a bit—silvery hair, olive skin—he was still a thin, very old man. "Thank you, thank you. You have no idea how happy you've made me. And my family will be ecstatic!" He squeezed her shoulders in affectionate excitement and then turned to hurry down the stairs. "I haven't got a minute to lose!" he said. "My plane leaves in an hour." She could barely keep up with him. In his office he picked up one of the new Gabriellas from the table, took out its voice box, and handed it to Rose. He put the one with the purple and yellow wires into the new doll and zipped her up. Rose put the traded voice-box into Gabby's limp body. "Hi-ya!" it said.

Mr. Edgar was all efficiency. He flung open his suitcase. Besides his one shirt and a toothbrush, there were two things in it: his family photograph and his U-shaped musical instrument.

"What is that, anyway?" Rose asked.

"You don't see them anymore," he replied mysteriously.

He packed his Gabriella into the suitcase, closed it, locked it.

"Where are you going now?" asked Rose.

"Home."

He was rushing around faster and faster. Rose wanted to grab him by the back of his ragged sweater and ask: How long will you be gone? How will we know whether the oracle gets there safely? Who are you really? Will we ever see you again?

"I'll write," said Mr. Edgar as he went out. The door slammed shut behind him.

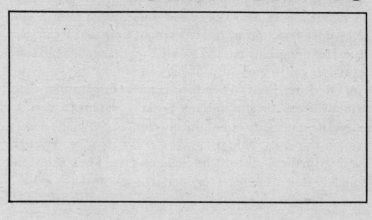

CHAPTER 18

"He's gone, and the oracle's gone, too," said Rose to nobody but herself. Here she was, standing in an abandoned office, staring at a bunch of old leaves in a wastebasket and listening to a roomful of talking dolls, all wailing "Ma-ma!"

Why had she let him talk her into it? Why? He had fooled her, utterly fooled her, with his tricks of light and persuasion.

The other side of her mind argued back: He didn't fool you; the oracle was truly his. It belonged to him, as if he were—well—Apollo himself. Rose wasn't sure she would mention this at home. Apollo in the disguise of an old man? Try telling that to your mother the next time she warns you not to talk to strangers.

Misery squeezed Rose's stomach. She would have to go home, and everybody, even Cindy, was going to be mad at her. Not Lucy, though. That was one good thing.

Now all the dolls in the workroom were crying. She giggled. Maybe she should take the whole lot home with her. Why not? Mr. Edgar certainly didn't want them. She poked around in the workroom until she found the big shopping bag he had carried in that morning. She shook it open, and a bit of paper fell out: the sales slip for the dozen dolls. They had cost Mr. Edgar quite a lot. Rose shoved the slip into her pocket. She might need to show it on her way out of the museum to prove she hadn't stolen the dolls. She dropped Gabby into the bag first and stuffed the rest of the dolls on top. Then she went quickly down the corridor, her arms clasped around the noisy bundle.

"How'd it go?" James's eager question stung Rose like alcohol on a fresh cut. She stood in the kitchen, her arms aching from holding the huge bag of dolls.

"He got her," she said to James. "The voice box, I mean. He said she was his and that he was taking her home. I'll tell you all about it."

Cindy was furious, and Rose couldn't blame her. "Rose Wilson! Twice now! I thought you were supposed to be an easy kid to watch—a piece of cake, compared with our friend James here! What am I going to tell your father? Do you need to be locked up? And where did those dolls come from?"

Rose let the bag fall onto a chair, and she sat down on a chair beside it. Lucy skipped in. "Did it work?" she asked. She looked from Rose, who said nothing, to James, who said nothing, to the bag of dolls. Lucy stood on tiptoe and peered into the bag. "Where'd you get all these? Is Gabby in here?"

"She's on the bottom, where she can't get lost," said Rose. Lucy practically stood on her head to paw through the bag. She drew out Gabby. "Well, sweetie!" she said to the doll. "You've had such a very scary time!" James caught Rose's eye and wrinkled his nose in faint distaste.

"She has her regular voice back," Rose said.

Lucy tipped and tilted her, producing the familiar sounds. "She doesn't tell the future anymore?" Lucy asked.

"No. Not anymore."

Lucy left the room. They heard the back door slam.

"The trick worked," Rose said to James. "The Russells brought her in. But Mr. Edgar ended up with her. He said the oracle, or the voice, was his all along." She began to sniff and then to cry. She felt entirely mixed up: She was sad, but at the same time she felt relieved of a burden and as light as air.

"Hey, don't cry!" James awkwardly handed her Kleenexes, which Cindy relayed to him from the other side of the sink.

"How come he said it was his?" asked James. "I knew we couldn't trust that guy."

"It *was* his. But he wasn't who he said he was."

"Now wait a minute!" Cindy interrupted. "Who did he say he was? What did he take? Looks to me like you came back with quite a bit more than you started out with. Who took what from whom?" she passed along a big pinch of Kleenexes.

"I just can't explain right now," said Rose.

"Well, at least you're here, when you do get ready to explain," said Cindy with a hint of sarcasm.

"I'm sorry if I made you worry again," said Rose.

"If? *If* you made me worry?"

"Where's Mr. Edgar?" asked James.

"He's gone. He said he was going straight to the airport. He's going home, to the Old World, wherever that is."

"That's too bad," said Cindy. "A cab driver came to the house a while ago and said he had instructions to leave a letter by Mr. Edgar's doorstep. Now he'll never get it."

"He probably won't care," said Rose. She had blotted her nose and eyes and was feeling better. She heard a jet crossing overhead, and she wondered if that was the one Mr. Edgar was on. Then she heard another, and soon after that a third. There was no way of telling which one was carrying him and the oracle.

Lucy slammed the back door and came into the kitchen again. "I tried her, and you're right. She won't say anything special now." Lucy was hugging Gabby and trying to look solemn, but Rose could tell that she wasn't particularly upset. Gabby had been a doll to her all along, and she still was.

"Something's wrong with the bush," Lucy added. "It's all dry and crackly under there."

The four of them went out to look at the bush. Even at a distance, Rose could see that it was smaller, shrunken. It was drying up. Rose and James crawled in. The smooth, oval leaves had turned brown around the edges. Some of them had withered to wrinkled little husks and were hanging by a thread of a stem. They began dropping off as the children crawled in. Rays of sun struck through the thinning branches and lit up the scrap of yellow rug and the heap of gifts, still stacked where they had been left. What a pile of junk, thought Rose. All their precious offerings.

"Guess we can take these back now," she said. She handed James his key chain—tarnished almost black from lying on the ground—and gathered up the turquoise handkerchief and the doll shoes and gilt scarf and the teapot.

"You've had quite a game out here, haven't you," said Cindy, surveying the motley collection.

"We're done with it now," said James.

"See, this trip this morning was part of it," Rose said to Cindy. "Part of the game. And since I got back all right, and now the game is over, do you have to tell my dad? You don't have to, do you? He'll be really upset."

"But Rose, you scared me half to death. And what if there's another time? Going off by yourself like that— that's no joke."

"I know. I wouldn't have done it if I didn't have to. There won't be any reason to do it again."

"Hi there! What's going on?" said a new voice. Rose turned around and saw Ron, the guy from the boat-renting dock at the pond. He wasn't talking to Rose or James or Lucy.

"Hi, Ron. Nothing much. You on your lunch break?" Rose saw a smile move all across Cindy's face, though her words were as cool as a cucumber. "Well, listen, Rose." Cindy turned back to her, but Rose could tell her attention was dwindling. "I'll think about it. Maybe I don't have to tell him. But only if you'll promise not to do it again. Promise? Swear on the Bible?"

"I promise. I never break promises."

Rose and James took the things from the cave and

walked back toward the house, leaving Cindy and Ron talking to each other on the grass. Lucy was still standing right beside them, listening to every word they said.

James turned when he and Rose reached the back door. "Hey, Lucy!" he called and whistled. "Come on. Help us with this stuff."

Rose was going to have a problem explaining the twelve extra dolls to her father. They were still gabbing away inside the shopping bag on the back porch. Cindy had put the bag out to get rid of the noise. Rose was going to have to think up something to tell him about them. And she was dreading his arrival even more because of something else. Her father must have called her mother in Iowa, and she was positive he was waiting to tell her the awful news in person when he got home. She was in quite a state by the time she heard his footsteps in the front hall.

"Hello?" he called out.

"Hi, Dad," she said, frozen at the table, scarcely moving her lips. Did he look sad or upset? She couldn't tell. He put down his briefcase, took off his jacket and hung it over the back of a kitchen chair, undid his tie and draped it over his jacket.

"I have some news for you," he said.

"Don't tell me yet!" she cried and put her hands over her ears.

"Rose? Heavens, what's the trouble?"

"It's bad news, isn't it? About Grandma Foley. Don't tell me what I don't want to hear!"

"It's anything but bad news. It's good news. I finally got through to your mother at the office today, and guess what? Your grandmother began talking again this morning, for the first time, and she sat up for a minute or two. It's very encouraging, very."

"You mean she's okay?"

"Not okay, but definitely improving. She has a good sense of who she is and where she is. So your mother is as happy as can be. Now, let's get Lucy. There's more to tell you both. Lucy?"

Lucy came down from their room. She had put Gabby in a fresh set of doll clothes and washed some of the smudges off her face.

"Lucy, Grandma Foley's getting better!" Rose exclaimed.

"Is Mom coming home?" asked Lucy.

"That's my other news," said their father. "Your mother is coming home tomorrow."

"Goody!" Lucy clapped her hands.

"She's going to fly back out to Iowa again in a few days, and you two will fly out with her. I'll come out, too, later on in August. You've always enjoyed your grandmother's little town in the summer—there are children to play with, and you can live in her house and visit her in the hospital while she recuperates. You should love it, especially you, Rose. You know what your mother said to me this morning? Grandma Foley told her once that you are her favorite companion, and your mother is sure she'd get well faster if you're there to see her."

"Oh, Dad!" Rose said. *Her favorite companion.* So that

was what the oracle had meant. The favorite companion was Rose.

"Can I be her favorite, too?" asked Lucy.

"Of course," said her father.

Rose smiled to herself, but she didn't bother to protest.

"In several months, if Grandma improves, and if we can find a suitable housekeeper, she may come to live with us. We'll take the second-floor rooms we talked about and we'll rearrange things nicely. The thing that worries me is having to tell Mr. Edgar that he has to move when the time comes. He seems quite alone in the world."

Rose and Lucy looked at each other.

"Now what do those faces mean?" asked their father.

"I think he's already moved out," said Rose.

"He's what?"

"He's gone on a trip."

"Without saying a word? That's unlikely."

Rose shrugged. She wasn't about to volunteer more.

"Let's go ring his bell and see if he's home," said Mr. Wilson, pushing open the back door. "What on earth is that?" A chorus of "Hi-ya" greeted him from the shopping bag.

"Mr. Edgar let me have those," said Rose. "There's twelve of them."

Mr. Wilson shook his head. "Oh, no! But what will we do with them?"

"I know!" said Lucy, putting her hand over her mouth and starting to giggle. "Let's give them all to Megan and her mom."

"We'll think about that later," said Mr. Wilson. They

went around to Mr. Edgar's front door. Beside the door-mat, just inside his entryway, was the envelope Cindy had told them about. But it had Mr. Wilson's name written on it. The handwriting matched the elegant hand that had written the card beside his bell: A. Edgar. The last thing he had said to Rose was that he would write. Rose had no idea he meant so soon.

Mr. Wilson opened the letter, and some smaller pieces of paper fell out. "You are right," he said when he had finished reading. "This is the most extraordinary thing. He has gone, and he is not coming back. We can either keep or get rid of his furniture. He has a collection that he is giving to the Children's Museum, but you two girls may go through it first and take whatever you wish. He has included a check for two months' rent. And—let's see—here's a note for James. It's just a string of numbers."

"Let me see." Rose took the note. On it was a series of two-digit numbers, with dashes between them. Three words were scrawled across the bottom: "With many thanks."

"I'll give this to James! Be right back!" Before her father could object, she jumped down Mr. Edgar's front stairs and ran up the street to James's house. She stood on the front porch, ringing the doorbell and peeking in the porch window. James was sitting in the living room, talking to himself. "I can't believe it!" he was saying to the curtains.

"James!"

"What are you doing here?" James pulled open the door. "Guess what?" he went on without waiting for her answer. "My mom came home a while ago and told me that my dad called her at work. He's not coming east this summer, but he's sending me a ticket to go out to California for a month. And stay with him! And so—" he stopped and swallowed and lost his voice.

"And so you will get to see him," Rose said slowly. "James, that's great. That's so great." She was almost whispering. She knew how long James had been waiting and hoping for this. "So the oracle was right! Your dad wasn't coming to see you; you are going to see him! You asked the wrong question!"

"I still wish I'd gotten those numbers down," James said gruffly.

"Oh my gosh, I forgot. That's what I came to give you! From Mr. Edgar." Rose handed him the note.

"You think this is the number?" he said.

"It must be. You'll just have to try it and find out. He said he wanted to thank you for killing the snake."

"But how did he get it?" James was puzzled.

"The same way we did, I guess," said Rose with a laugh.

"James?" called James's mother from the kitchen. "I'm ordering pizza for supper. Do you want pepperoni plain or pepperoni with onions?"

"If I win this lottery—" said James, ignoring her, "if I win it, I'll have enough money for airplane tickets to California every weekend from now till I'm a hundred!"

"James, pepperoni plain or with onions? If you don't answer me I'll order mushroom, and then you'll be sorry."

Mr. Wilson said he would order pizza for their supper, too. So many things were happening, he couldn't get organized to cook. They would surely want to clean the house a bit if their mother was coming home. Maybe they had better do a load of wash so that it wouldn't all be waiting for her.

"Can I go upstairs right now to look at what Mr. Edgar left behind?" Rose asked.

"Let's take a look after we've eaten," said her father.

"Can't Lucy and I go up while we're waiting for the pizza?"

"All right, if you're so anxious. Here's the spare key. But only stay for a minute. And don't lose the key."

Though there was no one to hear them, Rose and Lucy couldn't help talking in hushed voices and tiptoeing as they walked through the second-floor apartment. It was as if no one had ever lived there: Mr. Edgar's rooms were in perfect order, all except for the dining room. "Look at the plants," said Lucy. They had dropped their leaves, all over the floor and tables, and there was nothing left in the pots of earth but dry stems.

"Let's look at his collection," said Rose. She pushed open the door to the front room, and they scanned the shelves.

"Do you see anything you want?" asked Lucy.

"I might take one of those crystal balls," said Rose. "Who knows? Maybe it really works." She reached up to the shelf and lifted one down. It was heavy, and its polished surface gleamed. Rose set it on the floor and knelt beside it. She looked long and hard at the smoky glass, half daring its marbled depths to reveal a face, an event, a scene. It didn't. Rose sighed with relief. "I think we'll leave everything for the museum," she said firmly and replaced the ball on the shelf.

"I'm taking a deck of cards," said Lucy.

Rose was careful to lock the door behind them when they left.

Their mother's plane was due right after lunch the next day, and she was going to take a taxi home, rather than be met. So this was their last morning with Cindy. Lucy was pink with excitement. Cindy helped her tape a welcome-home picture to the refrigerator: a drawing of all the Wilsons and Grandma Foley and Gabby standing together beside a huge, peculiar-looking green bush.

Rose wanted to feel excited, too, but she found that the closer twelve o'clock came, the more nervous she got. Suddenly everything was changing: They wouldn't see James again until September, and she still hadn't told him all she wanted to about Mr. Edgar. Who could say if they would still be friends then? And how was it going to feel to have her mother back? Would she go right back to nagging Rose and never letting her go anyplace by herself? And then, what was Anita going to tell her? Or—worse—Cindy?

Rose couldn't get any lunch down at all: Her mouth was so dry, the bread stuck to her tongue. She sat in a stiff huddle at one end of the couch, feeling as if she were made of Tinker Toys. At last she heard a car with a rattling engine stop outside their house. A car door slammed, high heels sounded on the front steps—before her mother could ring the bell, Rose had thrown open the door and was hugging her with all her might.

"Mom, Mom," she cried, and right away she began to feel better.

"Mama!" Lucy came running up the hall, and Cindy came smiling behind her.

"Goodness, how I missed you!" said Mrs. Wilson. She gave Lucy a kiss on the top of her head and hugged Rose again. Then she drew back and gave Rose a careful look. "You know," she said, "you look taller and more grown-up than when I left. Isn't it funny how you notice these things after you've been away."

Everything would be all right, Rose knew then. Everything would be all right. How could she think that James would forget about her and Gabby while he was in California for a month? He was a real friend now. And pretty soon she would be seeing Grandma Foley and telling her all kinds of things. And she would probably be going swimming in the pool in Grandma's town. The pool was outdoors and was much nicer than the one at the Y. And one day—not this summer, but maybe the next—she'd go to the Island and see Ashley again. She knew she could count on that: It was as good as a promise. And who knew what would happen in the far, far future, when she was a grown-up? She might even take a trip to the Old World, and look up some of her friends.